LOVE ALWAYS PROTECTS

A GRACE HARBOR NOVEL

LUISA CISTERNA

INDEPENDENT

Love Always Protects – A Grace Harbor Novel

Copyright © 2024 by Luisa Cisterna

Cover design by Benjamin Cesar

Library and Archives Canada

ISBN 978-1-7780089-7-9 (Paperback)

To my late grandmother Helena Kemper.

CONTENTS

Chapter 1	1
Chapter 2	9
Chapter 3	17
Chapter 4	26
Chapter 5	35
Chapter 6	41
Chapter 7	47
Chapter 8	53
Chapter 9	60
Chapter 10	68
Chapter 11	75
Chapter 12	79
Chapter 13	86
Chapter 14	92
Chapter 15	100
Chapter 16	107
Chapter 17	114

Chapter 18   121

Chapter 19   127

Chapter 20   136

Chapter 21   145

Chapter 22   154

Chapter 23   162

Chapter 24   168

Chapter 25   174

Chapter 26   179

Chapter 27   186

Chapter 28   192

Chapter 29   196

Chapter 30   200

Chapter 31   206

Chapter 32   211

Chapter 33   218

CHAPTER 1

The sandcastle was crumbling. The foundation of vanity could never support it against the rising tide of reality and the force of despair. Some decisions were like gentle waves that licked around the sandcastle, causing minor damage. Others were tidal waves that swallowed up everything in their path.

And Nina's decision had the destructive power of a tidal wave.

Why had she believed in Anderson's promises of a happy and prosperous life together? Why had she trusted his flattering words that left her infatuated, even though she had known none of them was true? Other than her momentary blindness, Nina had no answers to these questions. Nothing would bring her relief, short of going back in time to prevent the worst mistake of her life, before she had said yes when he proposed, before she had put on her exquisite wedding gown, chosen by the groom. But Nina didn't have a time machine, so her only option was to swallow her present condition, a bitter pill, and face the future, hoping for miracles, hoping she could build something more solid than the sandcastle that was turning into a shapeless mound.

Nina, or Catarina, would trade all the luxury, the parties, and her fancy wardrobe for a moment of peace. All the glitzy gowns, designer shoes and purses, all of them were a reminder of who she wasn't. Like the green gown by one of the most coveted brands hanging on the silk-lined hanger on the closet door. It would snuggle her soft curves. With tears, Nina buried her face in her hands at the sight of the detestable dress in front of her.

She was discreet, even when she cried. A single wrong move or act of petulance could ignite Anderson's anger, like a ticking bomb. All it took was a spark, a slight flicker of what he considered his wife's misbehavior, to unleash his fiery temper. Confined to the walls of their home, Dr. Anderson Phillips' constant criticism of Nina poisoned the air she breathed, like carbon monoxide. No one could see it or smell it, but it was all too real for her. The blaming and shaming, like gas leaking unnoticed until it suffocated its victim, percolated through every cell of her body. Toxic. Lethal. Nina longed for fresh air to fill her lungs and detox her soul. Dad, I'm so sorry. How many times had she repeated this apology in her mind and heart?

As the waves pounded, Nina shrank each day, trying to go unnoticed by her husband. She cooked Anderson's meals, kept the house spotless and entertained his guests. Sometimes Nina hoped if she always did what was right, Anderson would change. He had already shown her he could be tender and kind. A few times, he had apologized for being harsh to her when he was under stress. He had given her flowers, and they'd travelled to the Bahamas. That was maybe four years ago, before he got busy with work at the hospital and meetings with the pharmaceutical company that funded his research.

Nina understood her obligations as the wife of a renowned plastic surgeon. She was still adapting to the expectations of Anderson's world. High society was a treacherous landscape. Dr. Anderson Phillips had warned his wife about the landmines on the way. And she had stepped on those mines several times, especially early in their marriage. Nina credited those missteps to her lack of sophistication. Certainly Anderson, ten years older than his wife, would guide her along the complicated social avenues of his world and show her the landmines. Nina soon discovered that Anderson deliberately made her step on the landmines to witness her public humiliation.

Before an important event, he would give her a briefing on the intricate relationships of the attendees. "Men will attend separate events with their wives and mistresses. It's your social responsibility to know who they are," Anderson once warned Nina. Despite her shock that such arrangements were real, she would memorize the names and relationships of those involved. At one philanthropic event, she had exchanged a few words with a dashing blonde in the ladies' restroom. As Nina said the woman's name, she felt a sinking feeling in her gut. It had taken her a few seconds to realize the blonde wasn't the mistress of the CEO of a tech company, but his wife. In horror, Nina tried to mend the situation, but it was too late. The woman stormed out of the ladies' room. Nina's legs shook, and she felt glued to the marble floor. She had been sure she had the right name. When her legs recovered, she maneuvered through the crowd like a boat in a thick fog. The blonde and Anderson were in a whispered conversation, their voices barely discernible over the live music. They stared at Nina for what seemed like a long time. Then the woman spun on her heels and disappeared through a nearby door. Anderson had gazed at his wife like a sheriff who'd found his fugitive. At home, he had hissed at her, spewing words Nina had never heard before. In that moment, she felt small, the familiar self-doubt consuming her. And she learned who Anderson was. Days later, she had made a similar mistake. It was then that she understood his intention to undermine her.

To the spectators of their lives, Nina and Anderson had the perfect marriage. He was charming and bright. She was beautiful, molded by his hands. They frequented the highest circles in town. Catarina Phillips had exclusive access to the finest boutiques, upscale salons, and fashion experts.

Women envied her. Men coveted her. And Nina hated herself. She was a fraud. A lie to others, but also to herself. Mainly to herself.

Hearing footsteps on the staircase, Nina rushed to the bathroom. She closed the door with caution and glanced at her reflection in the mirror above the spacious marble countertop with two sinks. She grabbed the hairbrush and smoothed out the strands that had fallen out of place. The mirror accused a tiny imperfection in her eyebrow, which Nina corrected at once with the eyebrow pencil.

The sound of the footsteps echoed through the bedroom. Nina's heart raced. She felt like a startled rabbit that had crossed paths with a cougar. Pulling her cell phone from the pocket of the silk robe, she sighed in relief. She wasn't late. Anderson had arrived early. Nina heard the rasp on the bathroom door and felt a surge of adrenaline.

"Catarina, I'm home." The deep, velvety voice, like a radio announcer's, reached Nina's ears, causing her stomach to burn.

"I'm almost ready. What time do you want to leave?" She controlled her tone as always. Neither too high nor too low. The wrong volume annoyed him. Over time, Nina had become skilled at fine-tuning it, like a pianist adjusting the keys.

"Didn't I say we'd leave at seven?" The smooth tone disappeared. His irritation leaked out from the door.

"Yes. Seven." Nina pressed her chest with both hands.

Her husband's grunt in response increased the burning in her stomach. The discomfort of hunger would last the length of the awards ceremony for the brightest minds of the Central Hospital. With her husband by her side, Nina would glide among the elegant guests. She would wear her best smile, her face covered in a lighter foundation to hide the caramel skin tone, just as Anderson liked. Taking a deep breath, Nina opened the bathroom door and stepped back into the spacious bedroom. A crisp, white duvet and charcoal throw pillows covered the king-sized bed. A modern black and white painting adorned the wall over the chestnut dresser. Nina's green dress on the hanger contrasted with the masculine palette of the room, like a huge caterpillar lost in a forest consumed by wildfire.

Anderson emerged from the walk-in closet, which was larger than her childhood bedroom. He tucked his tuxedo shirt into the black trousers, revealing toned arms and chest muscles underneath. He walked past his wife, kissed her cheek, and disappeared into the bathroom. Nina walked over to the dresser and pulled several tissues, wiping the spot where the kiss landed. She had a few spare minutes to reapply the foundation. Slipping the dress on, she felt the silky fabric drape over her body, fitting as snugly as a surgeon's glove. From the closet, she pulled out a pair of shoes from a collection of sandals, boots, and shoes organized by color on ten shelves.

Standing in front of the mirror on the closet wall, Nina struggled to zip up the back of the dress. Her eyes widened as the zipper refused to go up. Could the two slices of cake she had indulged in that afternoon had caused her sudden weight gain? Nina had skipped her portion of meat at lunch with two friends to treat herself to pastries in a little shop at the mall. She had planned the visit carefully. She had left the restaurant and driven to a suburban mall, taking precautions to avoid anyone who could inform Dr. Anderson of his wife's escapade.

The numbers on the scale had remained stable since Nina married. Before showering to get ready for the party today, she had weighed herself, just as she did every day at the same time. Of course there were normal daily weight fluctuations, and Anderson, as a doctor, should know that. But it wouldn't matter to him. His scientific knowledge vanished whenever Nina tried to explain her weight fluctuations. At those times, Anderson would grit his teeth and say, "Getting a little chunky." Then, he would kiss his wife and whisper in her ear, "Don't embarrass yourself." He wasn't at all concerned about her. He never was.

Nina grabbed her cell phone and opened the weight control app. The line graph showed a slight fluctuation, but no reason for alarm. Yet the zipper wouldn't go up. Her hands were sweaty as she made another futile attempt to pull it up.

Entering the closet, already buttoned up, Anderson looked at his wife. "What's wrong?" He gave Nina a suspicious look.

"Can you help me with the zipper?" That was an act of courage. Nina sucked in her belly, using her well-toned abdominal muscles. She smiled at

Anderson in the mirror, hoping to divert his attention from her waistline. The zipper slid up slowly, getting stuck at the waist. Tension. Anderson's condemning stare. The zipper went up. Done. Nina was secure in her green armor.

Anderson gave a light pat on his wife's buttock, making her feel like a horse in a stall. He turned his attention to the bow tie. "You've got a bit of a tummy showing."

"I'm about to get my period. A bit bloated." The curse of being married to a plastic surgeon took many forms. Nina had avoided her husband's scalpel, but not the filler needles. Her plump lips were someone else's, not hers. The pronounced cheekbones gave her a heavy look, but they were the trend among women in their social circle.

"Bad day for PMS." Anderson walked past her and disappeared into the maze of racks and shelves.

Nina swallowed hard. Tears would be a disaster. Slipping into the high-heeled shoes, she selected an evening clutch from a drawer. While transferring items from one purse to another, she heard her husband's lively conversation on the phone. He embodied politeness. He spoke with a polished, encouraging tone.

His charming voice had attracted Nina when they had met by chance at Central Hospital. As she roamed around the hospital, her heart felt heavy while she waited to hear about her father's heart surgery. Nina had lost her mom two years earlier. She couldn't stand the idea of losing her dad. The surgeon had said it was a routine operation and that the patient was strong. He had assured Nina she would receive a message on her cell phone when the surgery was over. Throughout the extended surgery, she kept on walking.

She had met Dr. Phillips next to a vending machine. In a white coat and with a bright smile, Anderson had introduced himself to the tall young woman with curly hair dressed in jeans and a t-shirt. Nina had put the coins in, which the machine had swallowed without dispensing the bag of chips. The doctor behind her had waited, swinging his stethoscope. Nina apologized and told him the machine wasn't working. They exchanged a few words, and Anderson got the chips for her and a protein bar for himself. They ate their snacks together by a large window and exchanged information about what they were doing at the hospital. The doctor's assurance lifted the weight on Nina's heart about her father's surgery. A female voice came through the speakers, notifying a code yellow. Dr. Phillips cut the conversation, explaining he needed to get back to work. He asked for Nina's contact information to get updates on her father's recovery. As Nina entered the O.R. waiting room, her feet clad in sneakers seemed to dance on the white floor, her smile radiating joy. The shy girl, who had never had a boyfriend, daydreamed about the doctor. She never expected him to call.

During her father's weeks of recovery, Anderson had called every other day. He visited the recovering patient in his modest home. Two months later, he asked Mr. Adams for permission to date Nina. She felt like she was floating on clouds of a summer morning. Six months later, she walked down the aisle.

And it was on their honeymoon that Nina started walking on eggshells.

She concealed her situation from her father. But Martin Adams knew his daughter. His surprise was evident when she visited him months after the wedding. Nina had straightened her curly hair and shed twenty pounds. She explained the struggle of buying stylish clothing with a waistline that had extra weight. She laughed and received a suspicious look from her father. About the hair, she said that women changed their hair all the time. "You always liked your curls," he had said with deep concern in his voice. Nina hadn't replied. Her mouth had felt dry, as if she had eaten sand. A memory of Dad pushing her on the swing flashed into her mind. "My angel with curly locks," he would say.

The years of marriage went by, and Nina distanced herself from her father. She and Anderson moved to a renovated mansion in Cleveland's upscale area. Mr. Adams rarely received invitations to his daughter's house. Anderson made excuses, explaining to his young wife that their new social circles were opposite to Mr. Adams's. The country club was the couple's weekend destination. Nina's father preferred the basketball team at the middle school and the church choir rehearsals. She made short and irregular calls to her dad. Mr. Adams didn't voice any complaints, but his tone suggested he had concerns about his daughter's marriage.

Over the years, Nina Adams had become Catarina Phillips. The reflection in the mirror showed a woman she didn't recognize.

"Ready?" the dry voice asked.

"Yes." Nina emerged from the closet and stood in front of her husband for the last inspection and approval.

Anderson gestured a circle in the air with his index finger, prompting Nina to spin around. "Earrings?"

Nina touched her ears with her manicured nails. How had she forgotten the diamond stud earrings Anderson had bought for that event? She rushed to the jewelry box on top of the dresser. She opened the golden lid and took out the earrings from the velvet-lined compartment. "Ready now."

Anderson nodded, smoothed his jacket, and left the room. Nina followed behind like a sad, dependent dog.

CHAPTER 2

The elegant couple drove towards the city's lit skyscrapers in a black Mercedes-Benz. An operetta played in the car. The soprano sang about a tragedy. Nina wanted to join the woman, scream at the top of her lungs about her own tragedy. An urge to roll down the window and cry for help overwhelmed her. She wanted to throw her hands into the chilly night air and denounce her jailor. Who would rescue her or pay her ransom? How many times had she pleaded with God to set her free? When was he going to answer her prayers? Was there a hotline in heaven for victims like her? In what order were the prayers answered, if ever?

Nina folded her hands on her lap. An act of defiance would land her in the psychiatric ward of the hospital. Anderson had done just that in their second year of marriage. Nina had packed her bags and threatened to leave. Two days of punishment in the hospital, with calming injections, had brought her back to her sad reality.

Nina shifted her focus away from the soprano's tragic performance and locked her eyes onto the vivid skyline of the city.

The brightest minds from Central Hospital would showcase their impressive achievements that night. A display of vanities. The money injected by the pharmaceutical industry would ensure an unforgettable party. Two top chefs would delight guests with their exquisite dishes, and Nina would barely touch them.

The valet, in a dark uniform and top hat, opened the Mercedes-Benz door, and Nina smiled at him. Anderson escorted her into the elegant, century-old hotel, the city's most traditional. More guests arrived and filled the grand entrance hall. Men in tuxedos escorted women in swishing gowns to the ballroom as directed by the hosts.

Nina thought of the soprano as she attempted to smile. She felt small despite her height in uncomfortable heels. It wasn't just the high ceiling and spacious surroundings that made her uneasy. She didn't belong. She never would. The caterpillar dress restricted her movements. Anderson's steely gaze intimidated her. The side slit on the long skirt revealed more of her leg than she desired. Everything was wrong, distorted.

Nina's stomach growled, protesting the hours without food. But she was more concerned about breathing. Anderson waved at a tall, grey-haired man. Nina recognized him as the CEO of Pharma Innovations, the event's sponsor.

Anderson released Nina's arm and headed towards the man. She saw them weave through the guests and vanish through a door. Anderson and Solos Dutra had a strange relationship. The powerful CEO had given her husband exquisite presents, like rare books and antique pieces of furniture. Nina suspected that the gesture was much more than mere generosity.

The string quartet played on a stage at the back of the ballroom, and the waiters passed by with trays of tall glasses, as if waltzing to the melody. Everything was well-coordinated, choreographed. Nina felt out of sync at these events, like a child in their first ballet recital. Anderson, however, moved around with the grace of an experienced dancer.

Nina disappeared amid the peacocks flaunting wealth and influence. A dark-skinned waiter lowered the tray and showed her delicate smoked salmon appetizers. With a discreet gesture, she turned down the food. Her breath would be a giveaway to Anderson. A different server presented her with a tray of vegetarian *hor d'oeuvre*. Nina grabbed one and popped it into her mouth. She glanced around, afraid of being caught by her husband.

Nina's challenge that night was to avoid a broken zipper while balancing on her feet. Her blood sugar was dropping. In distress, Nina called for another waiter. It was the same one serving the salmon appetizer. Her hands were sweaty, and her heart was racing, so she grabbed the appetizer and stuffed it into her mouth. She headed to the bathroom. If Anderson didn't intercept her, she would have time to rinse the smell off with mouthwash. She always carried a travel-size bottle for emergencies.

The mission was successful, and Nina sat for a moment in the upholstered chair of the enormous marble bathroom, waiting for her blood sugar to stabilize. When she left the bathroom, her breath was fresh again. It would be a long night, like all the ones she spent with Anderson. But soon the sun would rise, and Nina would have a few hours of rest from her husband's ever-accusing gaze.

***

"The dress made her look heavier." The petite woman in a pink and white tennis outfit set down the fork on the large plate and smoothed her pleated skirt.

"You can't even tell that she had liposuction." A redhead motioned for the server to come to their table.

Nina listened to Eliana and Giulia's comments, wondering what they would think if they knew her scale showed two extra pounds that morning. The hors d'oeuvres she'd indulged in at the party a few days ago had inflated her hips and waist. Nina could argue she was just bloated, but the tape measure confirmed the worst.

"Nina," Giulia said. "Samantha should've gone to your wonderful husband." The woman lifted her hands. "He has magic hands. I told Sam Dr. Douglas is a fraud."

Eliana shook her head. "Nina never comments on her husband's colleagues."

It was true. Nina kept her mouth shut because any inconvenient comment that reached Anderson's ears would serve as another reason to humiliate her. The weekly lunches at the country club were a huge test for Nina. Anderson insisted she met with Giulia and Eliana every week. Nina had a theory that her friends would report everything they saw and heard at the club to their husbands, who would report it to Anderson. He monitored Nina even in his absence.

Nina speared another shrimp with her fork. "Chef Robert outdid himself with this recipe." She placed the crustacean in her mouth, savoring the flavor, knowing she would have to leave the baby potatoes and carrots untouched.

The waiter appeared with more wine, which Nina declined. Eliana and Giulia sipped from their glasses as Nina drank her sparkling water with a slice of lime.

"I heard Patricia is separating from her husband." Eliana waved to a man at the next table, smiled at him, and received a blown kiss in return.

"Norman is a brute. He treats his wife like a housekeeper," Giulia said.

Nina brought the tall glass to her lips. What would her friends say if they knew the powerful Dr. Phillips, sculptor of women, treated his own wife like a housekeeper and cook? Of course, the two women would laugh in her face if Nina revealed what went on in their home. Who would believe that a man with a soft voice and impeccable manners could treat anyone badly, let alone his wife? After all, the women in their circle revered Dr. Anderson Phillips like he was a deity from ancient Greece.

Even in the air-conditioned restaurant at the country club, Nina felt sweat trickling down her back, soaking into her pristine white shirt. Her nerves were always on edge on Wednesdays. Despite enjoying the freedom of movement in tennis matches, what followed left her tense. The post-game lunches were never short on gossip.

Eliana covered her mouth with her long fingers and red nails. "I heard that the last straw was Norman hitting Patricia."

"If Dennis ever laid a hand on me—" Giulia crossed her arms and shook her head.

Ah, if they only knew there were other forms of violence. Nina snatched another shrimp from the plate before the waiter could clear it.

"Nina, you're so quiet today." Eliana gave her a typical smile, laden with rehearsed innocence.

"I'm worried about my father." It was better to steer the conversation to a safer topic.

"His heart?" Giulia asked.

"Not sure yet. He's lost weight and is feeling tired." The doctor had said she needed to run more tests. Her dad's phone call last week had caught her off guard. He rarely contacted his daughter. When he did, she always came up with an arsenal of excuses for why she hadn't called him. The last few times they spoke on the phone, they had argued about Anderson. She thought about confiding in her father, but she was afraid. Anderson had eavesdropped on one of these conversations and grabbed her by the wrist, the pain exploding in her arm. "I'm strong, Catarina," he had said while twisting her wrist.

Giulia patted Nina's hand, her diamond ring reflecting the sun that streamed through the restaurant's arched windows. "Everything will be fine."

"Yes." Eliana smiled, flashing her row of perfect teeth.

"Yes, yes, of course." Nina attempted to match her friends' tone of voice.

Eliana and Giulia devoured a crème brulé while Nina settled for a small bowl of fruit salad. No ice cream.

After a visit to the spa, the three women said their goodbye. Nina changed into black pants and a dark green blouse, got into her Volvo and headed to the beauty salon. The sauna had ruined her sleek hair. Her curls bounced as she maneuvered the car out of the parking lot. The Wednesday routine included a visit to Louis. Although Anderson had chosen him, Nina had grown fond of the hairstylist, who was French in name only. Despite being the son of Lebanese immigrants, he was well-liked by socialites. Louis was the only person Nina trusted enough to talk about less superficial topics.

To Nina's surprise and delight, the salon was nearly empty. The receptionist greeted her and led her to the chair reserved for Louis's clients.

"Would you like some coffee?" the young woman with short, layered hair asked.

"I'll have one of those chocolates." Nina pointed to the reception desk, where a crystal jar displayed the sweets.

The girl winked, went to the desk, and returned with a handful of small truffles wrapped in golden paper. Nina unwrapped one and popped it into her mouth, closing her eyes to savor the creamy texture of the chocolate. On her fourth truffle, Louis's image appeared in the mirror, his dark hair shinning with subtle highlights.

They exchanged a cheek kiss.

"Your favorite truffles." He smiled and slipped his hands into the pockets of the black apron.

Nina spun in the chair. "Mm-hm."

"Enjoy." His smile brightened his olive complexion.

This was a special moment for Nina. She tried to forget the tape measure and the scale.

Louis washed her thick hair, massaging the scalp. Nina had a foot massage during her hair treatment. Louis disappeared through a door and returned with a bottle in his hand.

"Just arrived today." He opened the lid and held the cream up to Nina's nose.

"Delightful." She inhaled the fragrance.

The beauty ritual continued for an hour. With her hair hydrated and damp, Nina returned to the chair in front of the mirror. Her curls bounced like little brown springs. Soon, they would disappear under the heat of the flatiron. Louis ran his fingers through his client's curls from behind. Nina could see the sadness on his face. But that was the agreement. Or rather, Anderson's orders—straight hair.

As the curls vanished, Nina's initial joy faded. The taste of the truffles disappeared. Nina disappeared. In her place, Catarina returned. "Anderson still thinks straight hair suits me better."

Louis smoothed another strand and nodded. His expression showed empathy, not condemnation. Every Wednesday, the conversation between the hair stylist and his client returned to the subject of curly hair. Nina would only shrug.

With her hair straight as a plank, she said goodbye to Louis. Back in the Volvo, Nina looked at herself in the rear-view mirror. Catarina was back.

Her cell phone buzzed in the purse. The screen showed her father's image. Nina's fingers trembled as she answered the call. "Dad, are you okay? Did you see the doctor?"

"I did."

"And?"

"She wants more tests."

More tests again? That was never a good thing. "Why?"

"Because everything came back normal, but I still feel tired."

Her father's complaints seemed vague to Nina. He was a healthy man. The last visit to the cardiologist had shown that everything was fine. Martin's two calls in one week hinted at a change. His voice had become sluggish. He complained of fatigue and had reduced his basketball practice hours. Nina wanted to visit him, to have dinner with him, but Anderson would object. It was the night of his roast beef with horseradish sauce. He claimed that only Nina's was any good. A great compliment from someone who always belittled her. He enjoyed seeing Nina in the kitchen each night. It was a matter of control for him.

"I'd like to visit you, Dad, but—"

"It's Anderson's lobster night."

How did he remember Anderson's ritual? Nina had mentioned her husband's dietary habit to her dad once or twice. "Roast beef."

"I see."

Nina found it strange that her father's tone lacked its usual irritation when talking about his son-in-law. Instead, he sounded as if he needed extra energy to speak. What if he was hiding something and his health was deteriorating? If she visited him and stayed only half an hour, she would have time to return home and prepare Anderson's supper. The meat was marinating, and the potatoes cut. Taking the express highway would save her time, considering the rush hour.

"I'll drop by, Dad."

"Now? What about Anderson's dinner?"

"Don't worry."

In six years of marriage, this was Nina's most rebellious act, aside from the time she'd threatened to leave home. Her father needed her.

The risk was worth it, even if her husband's roast beef wasn't ready on time.

CHAPTER 3

The tree-lined street stretched ahead. The branches cast shadows on rows of modest houses with faded paint. Nina parked in front of the house with chipped white shutters. The creamy yellow of the stucco had faded to the color of margarine. The afternoon rays of the sun exposed the tired state of Nina's family home. She opened the picket fence gate, catching the attention of a neighbor watering her plants with a hose. Nina waved, receiving a nod in return. The middle-aged woman turned away and sprayed water on the shrubs along her stretch of sidewalk. A dog barked somewhere in the backyard, and another responded.

Nina rang the doorbell. She started timing the half-hour she would spend with her father. Her internal clock was infallible.

Mr. Adams opened the door. Nina gasped. Her father's button-up shirt and jeans hung from his gaunt body. His face was sunken and worn, showing signs of exhaustion. "Dad." She wrapped her arms around him, her hands feeling the protruding bones on his back.

"Nina." He sighed.

They stepped into the living room. Memories washed over Nina as she gazed at the shabby furniture that once was fashionable. Her mother had chosen each piece when Nina was about nine. That was the year her dad joined the police force, and her mother became the principal of the elementary school down the street. In that room, Nina had played with dolls on the couch, lain on the carpet with her cat Penelope, ate cookies and watched *Powerpuff Girls* and *SpongeBob* on TV. She could almost hear pots clanging from the kitchen and smell the roast chicken that mom prepared in a rotisserie oven.

Nina sat beside her father, placing her designer purse on the floor. "So, what did the doctor say?"

Martin Adams shrugged. "What I told you; more tests."

"What exactly are you feeling?" Nina's heart raced. Things were not right.

He leaned back on the throw pillows. "I could say I'm in pain, but that's not it." He tapped his chest.

Nina's temples throbbed. Worry and guilt swirled in her chest. "Your heart? Dad? What are you hiding?"

Her father shook his head. "I told you. The doctor can't find anything wrong. She will run more tests. What I feel is an emptiness in my chest."

Nina glanced at her father's graying hair, now so fine that the scalp was visible. She looked back into his brown eyes. Depression? Loneliness? Martin Adams was a widower, and his daughter lived far (well, not that far, but she was distant). Perhaps his loneliness caused the depression. "Any major issues bothering you?"

"If you're talking about my work with the basketball team or the church, no." His shoulder sagged.

"Then what?" Looking into her father's eyes, Nina wished she hadn't asked that question. His eyes were wells of deep sadness.

"Nina, I can't bear to see you like this anymore."

Her chest convulsed with guilt and fear. "I'm alright, Dad." Nina had come here to check on her father, not discuss her predicaments. Any misstep would cause Anderson to boil over with anger, spewing it towards her like lava. She glanced at the clock on the wall. Tick, tack. Anderson's roast beef was waiting.

Martin sat up straight. "Let's be direct. We've been beating around this topic for six years. You're dying, Nina. I don't recognize my daughter. If your mother raised from the dead, she wouldn't recognize you either." Martin reached out his hand, gesturing toward his daughter.

Nina grabbed her purse off the floor and stood up. "Dad, I'm the same person." Twenty minutes had already passed. The clock on the wall seemed to melt like Salvador Dali's surreal clock.

"Where are you going?" Martin looked up, searching for his daughter's gaze.

She crossed the small room in a few steps. "I need to go." Her finger trembled as she turned the doorknob.

Martin followed her. "The roast beef."

Nina looked at her father. "You don't understand."

"I'm a retired police officer and understand abuse. I've seen things, terrible things. Working with children, parents, mothers, families, I know very well what happens when we don't confront abuse."

Nina let out a nervous laugh. Anderson would disapprove of the tone. "What are you talking about? What abuse?" She stretched out her arms and lifted her face. "Look, Dad. No bruises, no scars, nothing."

"Nina, abuse isn't just physical violence. I've watched my beautiful girl die slowly for six years." His thin hand stroked his daughter's smooth hair. "This isn't you. These clothes. None of this is you."

"Dad, why are you saying these things?" She felt dizzy and wanted to go home, like a hostage suffering from Stockholm Syndrome. Nina loved her father. But Anderson would be waiting. The clock on the wall melted some more.

"Nina, Dr. Kaur said I'm depressed."

"Depression is treatable. Did she prescribe any medication?"

"Medication won't cure me."

"Is that what the doctor said? She's wrong." Beads of sweat formed on Nina's neck. It would make her hair frizzy. She wiped the sweat from her neck with her long fingers.

"She didn't say that. I know it. I'm dying slowly, too, watching your life slip away in the hands of that man who lives a lie."

Five more minutes and Nina would never make it home on time. "Dad, you sound like Aunt Mildred, making a mountain out of a molehill. I'm okay and you'll be, too." Three minutes.

"This isn't drama." Martin gripped his daughter's shoulders. "I'll support you if you leave him. You can start over, go back to college to complete your Social Work degree. That has always been your dream."

Anderson had called Nina a supporter of losers when she shared her dream of becoming a social worker before they married. She shook her head. "It's not that simple." Two more minutes.

"Nina, my beautiful girl, please. Leave this nightmare." A strangled sound escaped his lips. "I pray for you every day."

Nina clenched her jaw and looked at her dad. "God doesn't answer my phone call." She regretted the sarcasm when her father's eyes reddened. To be fair, she had made her bed. The choice of marrying Anderson was her own, despite her father's reluctance to accept their speedy dating. Now, her father, a man of faith, was suggesting divorce? How many times had she heard from the pastor and her parents that God didn't like divorce? Nina needed to try harder, make her marriage work. If she did everything right, she and Anderson wouldn't have conflicts. One minute. "I need to go." Nina turned the doorknob and opened the door, stepping out onto the porch.

"Nina, God will answer. Maybe he already did." Holding onto her shoulders again, he furrowed his brow. "He has plans for your prosperity, not plans for your harm. Plans of hope and a future, Nina."

The Bible verses seemed like snowflakes in early spring, falling to the ground and melting right away. Nina saw no prosperity, hope or a future on the horizon. God's hotline was busy. *Your call will be answered in... an eternity.* Nina swallowed hard and ran to the car, tears streamed down her face the entire way to the bridge, where a bus accident had stalled traffic.

***

A fire truck blared the sirens as it maneuvered through a sea of red taillights. Nina looked at the electronic dashboard of the Volvo. She had ten minutes to escape the chaos and reach her house. She thought of ways to get dinner on the table on time if she arrived a few minutes late. Increasing the oven temperature would speed up the cooking process, but it could dry out the meat. Leaving the meat undercooked would fuel up Anderson's temper. If she served an appetizer first, he would suspect something was wrong.

The tow truck lifted the bus. Nina would have time after all.

As she waited for the police to reopen another lane, Nina mentally went over the recipe for the horseradish sauce, Anderson's favorite. She kept several jars of horseradish paste in the pantry, so it would never run out. The last time Nina made this grave mistake, Anderson had sent her to sleep in the guest room. He called Eliana the next day and canceled a dinner Nina was hosting for her and her husband. The gossip spread through the club that day and came back to Nina with a vengeance, through Eliana's voice. The rumor was that Nina had had a breakdown. Nina never understood why the lack of horseradish turned into gossiping about her mental state. The following week, she tried to explain to her friends that she'd had a severe migraine that drove her crazy. She knew better than to contradict Anderson, so she had hoped the spin would work and silence the busybodies.

The police opened another lane on the bridge. Nina tapped her fingers on the soft leather steering wheel, trying to release her tension. Her father's words came back like a cold dash of water. Nina had never expected that from him. He always said meddling in someone else's marriage was wrong, the very mistake he was making. Hearing quoted Bible verses only made Nina more frustrated. Hope. Future. In her dreams!

The truck towed the bus, and the traffic started moving. Four more traffic lights, and Nina would be home, in her kitchen, taking the roast beef out of the fridge. She pressed the accelerator as her lane cleared. She turned the next corner and breathed a sigh of relief at the light traffic. Her relief didn't last long—there was a car parked in front of her house. Well, maybe someone was visiting the neighbor next door.

With trembling fingers, Nina tapped on the remote control and the garage door rolled up. Her heart skipped a beat and then raced, like a sprinter at the starting signal. Anderson's Mercedes was already inside, a menacing figure in the dark. Nina parked the car and got out, fumbling with the straps of the purse and the gym bag, her breath coming in short, uneven gasps.

In the mudroom, she plopped the bag in the coat closet. Running her nails through her hair, Nina ran to the kitchen. She took the meat out of the fridge, turned on the over just a little higher than usual and placed the Dutch pot in. She prepared a tray with Anderson's favorite cocktail and armed herself with her best smile.

Anderson's gaze was the first thing she saw when she entered the living room—furious, almost apoplectic. He stood up from the armchair and kissed his wife's cheek. "We need another cocktail, don't we, Nina?"

It was then that she saw the guest, Solos Dutra. The tall man in his mid-forties was the reason Anderson had kissed her and not knocked the tray.

"Oh, sorry. Of course." Nina greeted Dutra, holding back the tears. She wouldn't dare hint she wasn't expecting a guest for supper.

"Anderson insisted you were always ready for guests." The man with salt and pepper hair smiled at Nina, then turned to Anderson to continue their conversation.

"I'm glad you accepted the invitation." Balancing the tall glass on the tray, she went back to the kitchen, sure Dutra hadn't heard her.

The oven beeped, informing her it had reached the right temperature. Nina refreshed Anderson's drink and prepared another one for the guest.

Back in the living room, she served the drinks. Both men, legs crossed, paid Nina as much attention as they would a server in a fast-food restaurant.

Nina smiled, though she wanted to scream and run. The men began talking about new drugs and things Nina didn't care to understand. She retreated to the safety of the kitchen. The guest would serve as a shield, protecting her from her Anderson's immediate anger.

When the meat was in the oven and the asparagus washed, Anderson came in and leaned his muscular body against Nina's back, pressing her against the countertop. He held her waist with both hands and applied light pressure. "This dinner had better be spectacular."

She cringed. "It will be."

"Where were you, Catarina?" His moist breath spread on her neck.

"I needed to see my father." Her hips hurt against the granite countertop.

Anderson griped her waist harder. "Right before dinnertime?"

Beads of sweat formed on the back of her neck. "It was much earlier, but there was an accident on the—"

"No more excuses." He let go of her waist.

Her ouch came out as a sob. She held on to the countertop, looking down. "It won't happen again."

He kissed Nina's neck. "Better not."

Anderson left the kitchen, and Nina heard his cheerful voice telling the guest how incredible the roast beef was turning out. As she arranged the asparagus on a baking sheet, she swallowed the bitter lump rising in her throat. Her father's words echoed in her mind, bringing a sharp pain to her temple. *Get out of this nightmare.* But how? How could she leave home, and where would she go? Moving in with her father would be another nightmare. Nina knew this too well. She had tried leaving home before and ended up in the psychiatric ward. Anderson began spreading rumors that she was depressed and had attempted suicide. Eliana and Giulia hadn't made comments, but their eyes on Nina carried judgement. The worst part was watching Anderson play the victim. When Nina came back from the hospital, she already had an appointment scheduled with a psychologist. At first, she thought it was a good idea to have someone to talk to, but when she discovered that Dr. Katso was Anderson's friend, she clammed up. In those sessions, she talked about her weight issues and some childhood traumas she invented, like when her cat, Penelope, was run over by a motorbike.

At the table, Anderson and his guest discussed work matters while Nina darted back and forth, making sure the meal was as perfect as her husband expected. During dessert, which Nina didn't touch after seeing the warning in Anderson's eyes, she allowed herself to think about running away. The first hurdle would be money. They had joint bank accounts, and Anderson controlled every penny. He paid for and monitored every credit card purchase. At any minor slip in her spending habits, he would freeze the account and cards. Her father lived on a meager pension as a retired police officer. The house was paid off, but his income only covered the basics. Nina would have to figure out a way to get money to escape. After that, she could find a job far away from here and maybe even go back to school in the future.

"Catarina, the coffee."

Nina snapped out of her thoughts and apologized. "Cappuccino or espresso?" She tried to make eye contact with Anderson, who sat at the end of the long mahogany table. The wall of the dining-room seemed to close in on her. The room felt cramped and suffocating. Nina hated the decoration, mid-century with contemporary touches.

"Espresso for me," Dutra said.

"The same for me." Anderson continued chatting with the guest, his soft laugh permeating the otherwise serious conversation.

It was only much later, after Dutra had left and Anderson was finally asleep, that Nina allowed herself to think about her plan. With her arm over her head in the dark bedroom, she considered the options. Anderson mumbled something and turned to his side. Nina kept her breathing shallow while her mind ran wildly.

At five in the morning, Nina left the house for her morning run before making her husband's breakfast. Crucial parts of her plan were already taking shape.

Two weeks. If everything aligned, Nina would be free.

CHAPTER 4

Perfectionists hated change, and Nina used this to her advantage. Anderson's routine was as predictable as a rooster's crow. In the following days, she implemented part of the plan to leave Anderson for good. She took a suitcase with a few clothes to her father's house, after her midweek visit to Louis to flatten the already-unmanageable curly locks.

The day before, Nina had stopped by a Walmart, bought a suitcase and a backpack, two pairs of jeans, some neutral color T-shirts, cheap sneakers and a hoodie. Then she'd called her father, briefly explaining that she needed to drop off a few items at his place. He had looked at her with suspicion when Nina arrived, but had remained quiet as he helped her tuck away the purchase in the bedroom. As a seasoned police officer, he might have suspected something important was about to happen. His furrowed brow had relaxed when Nina said she was coming for the suitcase in a couple of weeks.

With the first step of the plan resolved, Nina devised what would come next. The financial issue was the most complicated to solve. Worst-case scenario, Nina would ask her father for a loan. Maybe he had some savings. At the beginning of the marriage, Nina had felt relieved that Anderson managed their finances. She had come from a modest background, and her salary as a hotel receptionist barely covered part of her studies and general expenses. She lived with her father rent-free at the time. In their first year of marriage, Nina and Anderson lived well, despite some limitations. Once he completed his residency, their bank account balance grew. When

Dutra entered Anderson's life three years later, a sudden influx of money followed. The new plastic surgeon quickly became popular among the city's wealthy residents, who invited him to their social gatherings. Women filled Dr. Phillips' schedule, eager to let him sculp their breasts, legs and faces.

Anderson monitored his money with the precision of an accountant. With her credit card and account under her husband's supervision, Nina avoided spending on anything that Anderson deemed unnecessary. Once, Nina bought a collection of crystal figurines. She loved the small sea creatures crafted with care. The seahorse, the starfish and the orca had been her favorite. Nina felt like the character of Tennessee Williams' play with her beloved glass menagerie—isolated in her fragile environment. When Anderson saw the statement with the expense, he exploded and vowed to shatter the collection. To protect herself and the tiny creatures, Nina returned them to evade Anderson's anger. Early in her marriage, she realized that her shopping should be restricted to groceries and beauty products.

On the day that Anderson discovered the purchase of the figures, he cut Nina's credit card to pieces. Nina had learned another life lesson under Anderson's tyranny.

A week before her escape, she doubted she could execute her plan. She did her best to avoid Anderson's anger. One night, he asked her why she was being so well-behaved.

The next day, Nina burned his toast on purpose.

Nina's anxiety grew as the days went by. Her father sent her a message asking when she would pick up the suitcase. Nina replied she didn't have a specific date. Then, he sent her another message saying that if she needed anything, anything at all, even money, he could help her. A faint sense of relief gave her the courage to continue.

On the last weekend at home, Nina felt like she was escaping Alcatraz. Anything could go wrong. She was livid when Anderson announced he had invited Solos Dutra and his wife over for dinner. It was already four o'clock, and she needed to find room in her mind to come up with a suitable menu. Frantically, Nina searched the kitchen, opening both the pantry and fridge, trying to come up with ideas.

Late afternoon, Anderson marched into the kitchen and stared at her with his steely eyes. "Last time, the asparagus was overcooked. Don't let that happen again."

Anderson's cell phone buzzed in the pocket of his trousers, and he turned his back to Nina as he answered it. She looked at the knife as she was chopping onions and imagined what it would be like to plunge the blade into his chest. The tears streamed down her face. Anderson disappeared into the hallway, laughing at something the person on the line said.

Nina dried her tears with the dish towel. With the pork chops in the oven, she had ten minutes to shower and get ready. The outfit, a pair of silk pants and a patterned tunic, was already hanging on the closet door. Anderson's choice.

At eight o'clock sharp, Nina was elegantly dressed and ready for her guests. The doorbell rang ten minutes later. She opened the door for Soros Dutra and Milena, his third or fourth wife. The women's ages appeared to decrease with each new marriage. Tall and blonde, Milena entered the living room as if walking down a runway. She twirled on the Persian rug, looking up at the ceiling with ornate crown molding.

"Wow, fancy!" She chewed her gum with gusto, as if to extract the last drop of minty flavor.

Nina smiled at the woman, who made more enthusiastic comments about the décor. Solos Dutra didn't seem too impressed with his sexy wife. She wore a short slip dress with an open back. Nina wondered what imperfections Anderson would find in the young woman's lean body with flawless skin.

As on cue, Anderson entered the room with a politician's smile and greeted the couple, ignoring his own wife. "I'm delighted to have you in my home."

My home. Never our home. Nina knew her husband's statement was meant to hurt her, to put her in her place as his housekeeper and puppet.

"Your home looks like that museum we visited in Florence." Milena clutched her husband's arm. "What was it called again, honey bunny?"

"Palazzo Vecchio, dear." The corner of Dutra's mouth twitched.

"That one, that one." She giggled, her red lips revealing white teeth. "My honey bunny knows everything."

Anderson nodded and invited the couple to sit down. Milena chatted about other museums they visited in Europe, always turning to her impatient husband for help to pronounce their names.

Nina stood by the sofa. She watched her husband laughing at Milena's babbling and Dutra's twitching mouth. When the woman took a breath, Nina said:

"If you'll excuse me, I'll grab the drinks."

Milena leaped from the couch. "Oh, can I come join you? I'd love to see your kitchen. Besides, these two," she pointed at the men, "will talk non-stop about business, drugs, research and all. So boring." She blew a kiss to her husband, and he smiled, the twitch intensifying.

Nina didn't have time to respond, and the guest was already at her side.

"How long have you been married?" Milena asked as they crossed the dining area to the kitchen.

"Six years." Nina took out the tall glasses from the cupboard and arranged them on a silver tray.

Milena sat on the island, swinging her long legs. "Wow, I don't know if I want to be married that long."

Nina filled the glasses with a yellow cocktail and garnished the rims with fruit pieces skewered on sticks. "Why not?"

The woman leaned forward and lowered her voice. "Solos' friends mistreat their wives. They have no respect for them." She scoffed and examined her long, red nails. "It only takes some time for Solos to send me to the kitchen and hand me a mop. I'm his little distraction now, but not for long. I see the signs."

The woman's comment caught Nina off guard with its raw honesty and realism. "How do you feel about this?"

Milena shrugged. "It's been a fair agreement so far. I'm his trophy wife, and he's my source of income. When the rules of the game changes, I'm out."

Nina balanced the tray with the tall glasses. Her body felt hot and clammy, like she was going through menopause. Marriages around her seemed to be all about performance and façade. Her ideal of love felt like a distant fantasy. Would it be possible to experience real intimacy in marriage? Nina thought so when she remembered her parents together. They had gone through highs and lows, but they had forged an unbreakable bond of commitment and love.

Carrying the tray, Nina headed toward the living room, her mind a whirlwind of thoughts. Milena followed her, the heels of her shoes clicking on the hardwood floor. The young woman took her drink and sat on the arm of her husband's armchair. "So, did you talk about money, or did you talk a little about me, too?"

Nina noticed Anderson stiffen his back when she sat next to him. He laughed at Milena's comment and said they'd only talked about boring things.

At dinner, Milena steered the conversation toward cosmetic procedures, delighting Anderson, who flaunted his expertise as if lecturing medical residents. Nina made several trips to the kitchen and back, bringing dish after dish. When dessert was served, she was exhausted from hearing about liposuction, fillers, nipping and tucking.

The men returned to the living room after the meal while Nina tidied up the kitchen.

Milena took her place by the counter, sipping from a flute of Prosecco. "Don't you get tired? I'm exhausted looking at you."

Nina sighed as she scraped the leftover food from the dishes into the sink. "Sometimes."

"Dr. Phillips doesn't pay much attention to you, does he?" She swirled the flute in her hands.

The young trophy wife has no filter. "He is a very busy man."

Milena settled the empty flute on the granite top. "Does he abuse you?"

Nina's eyes widened, and she closed the double-door refrigerator, where she had stored several food containers. "He has never laid a finger on me." Well, if Nina didn't count the times he had squeezed her wrists, had pushed her against the wall or pressed the back of her neck.

The young woman moved closer, the straps of her dress slipping down her shoulders. "Do you have access to the bank accounts, cards, those things?"

"Yes, I do." Nina twisted her fingers. Sweat dripped down her back under the tunic.

"Can you use them as you please?"

"We don't like spending on unnecessary things."

Milena scanned the modern kitchen. "Does he control your spending?"

What would she say? "It's a mutual agreement."

Milena held Nina's wrist. "Domestic abuse has many forms: manipulation, control, and threats." She stared at Nina. "It doesn't take a genius to notice something very wrong going on between you two. I can sniff abuse miles away. I come from a line of abused women: grandma, mother. Myself." She released Nina's arm. "Where's the toilet?"

Without waiting for an answer, the woman disappeared down the hallway. Nina heard the clicking heels and held back tears. Does everyone see this, and have I been blind for six years? Dad, Louis, even Milena?

Nina returned to the living room with a tray of coffee cups just in time to hear the word bribery coming from her husband's mouth. She saw Dutra's expression harden. To Nina's relief, Milena entered the room describing the guest bathroom, talking about the copper faucets and the marble floor. The momentary tension dissolved, at least on the surface. The guests had coffee, and half an hour later, they said their goodbyes. Milena invited Nina to go shopping next week. Anderson thanked her for the invitation and said his wife would go when she wasn't so busy.

Milena glanced at Nina. She was about to say something when Anderson said:

"Well, have a good night."

He opened the front door. Nina watched as the couple walked down the driveway toward their Mercedes. She felt an urge to take off her uncomfortable shoes and run. Run, turn the corner, run some more into the night until she could no longer see Anderson and his detestable house. She had a plan, but the money part was still unresolved.

Milena was right. Anderson controlled everything. And Nina had to leave.

Anderson closed the door and retreated to his office. Not a sarcastic thank-you, nothing. After cleaning the kitchen, Nina went to bed. She reviewed her plan in the dark bedroom.

***

Two days before leaving her home for good, Nina considered revealing the plan to her father. Her wallet had a few bills, which she used for minor expenses. But the plan would be costly. Without money, she wouldn't even make it to downtown if she took a taxi.

To relieve the tension, Nina stepped into the closet to find things to do. Anderson had already hinted that her shirts were wrinkled. Nina took out six hangers and carried the shirts to the laundry area. Ironing them would be Nina's last good deed to her husband. Ironic that in her last days at home, she gravitated toward arranging things for him.

While hanging the shirts, her nails got stuck in a gap at the back of the closet. Letting out a moan, she examined a broken nail. She had one more task before preparing supper—fixing her nail. Anderson detested women with unkempt nails, especially if the woman was his wife.

Pushing the hangers aside, Nina inspected the gap in the drywall, a sliding door the size of a computer monitor. That was news to her. She recalled that during the home renovation, Anderson had handled the closet design. Nina had thought it was odd, but she didn't want to cause any fuss about the number of shelves or rods the carpenter would install.

She slid the door open. Inside, a small security box sat nestled in the compartment in the wall. The key was in the lock. With trembling fingers, Nina turned it and opened the metal lid.

In one hour, Anderson would arrive home. She had supper to prepare. Her curiosity had to wait. But a leather portfolio folder caught her attention. Anderson had a habit of storing personal documents in a safe in his office to protect them from fire and prying eyes. Why was that folder hidden in a security box in the closet?

Nina pulled the folder, looking around as if someone was watching. She opened it and fumbled with the contents. She pulled the stack of documents and shuffled through them. Her eyes darted over numbers and names she didn't recognize, but one: Solos Dutra. She remembered hearing the word bribery from Anderson's lips the day Dutra and Milena came over for supper. Did those papers have anything to do with it?

She returned the documents to the folder and slid her hand through the pocket of the folder. Her fingers brushed against something she quickly recognized. She pulled out a bundle of cash. A rubber band secured the money. Her mind raced. Why did Anderson hide it there? The sight of the money sent a chill down her spine. That was the missing piece of her plan.

Could she... should she get the money now? What if Anderson noticed it was gone?

Nina ran her index finger along the crisp edges of the bills, and considered if she should return the money to the safety box. Two more days.

If the money was gone, she'd find another way.

CHAPTER 5

One hour. Anderson would arrive in one hour and catch Nina rummaging through his closet. With her heart racing, she looked at the bundle of cash in her hands. Was that an answer to her feeble prayers? Or her dad's? Nina reined in her enthusiasm. The money could be gone any time.

Running her thumb along the side of the bundle, Nina estimated the amount could take her far away from Anderson. More than ever, she needed to be far away. Anderson would accuse her of leaving home and stealing his money. One crime justified the other. Six years living for her husband, obeying him, humiliating herself, denying herself, would end. Milena was right. Anderson manipulated her, tortured her with his lethal words. Why had Nina taken so long to act? She knew the answer: fear. The longer she stayed with him, the stronger her fear became. She needed to break the bondage, no matter the cost.

Forty minutes. She put everything back in the compartment behind her husband's shirts and slid the door closed. Taking the money now would create more problems than not, if Anderson found out. If the money was gone when the time came for her to leave, her dad could lend her some. That's what he had said. She would find a job, pay him back.

Nina hurried to the bathroom. She grabbed a nail file, polish remover, and nail polish from the vanity drawer. Within a few minutes, she had fixed her broken nail.

Anderson arrived at seven as Nina was taking dinner out of the oven. He passed through the kitchen, gave Nina a pat on the butt, and went upstairs to the bedroom. She hated that pat. Hated it. She calmed the fireball that surged up her esophagus with a glass of ice-cold water. Two more days. No more pats on the butt.

At the dinner table, Anderson kept silent. No chiding, no complaints. He was unusually distracted by his phone. Something was off. Did Anderson suspect something? Was there a hidden camera in the bedroom and closet? Panic gripped her like tentacles. She glanced at Anderson over her plate with four Brussel sprouts and a small portion of fish. His expression was unreadable, but his lips were pale. Maybe he was coming down with a cold or something. He didn't seem to notice his wife across the long dining-table, not even to humiliate her.

Anderson didn't finish the fish fillet and left the table, heading straight to his study, locking himself in. Relief replaced Nina's fear. She busied herself cleaning the kitchen, thinking about the money. For the next hour, Anderson remained in the study. Nina dried the last pot and put it away. The rhythmic hum of the dishwasher kept her company as she wiped the countertop.

She opened the pantry and took an inventory of the cans and jars: tomato sauce, olives, capers. There were only two jars of horseradish sauce. Not for long. She allowed herself a little smirk. Nina had included that part in her plan. A detail that would be her special farewell to Anderson. Her departure signature. A revengeful goodbye.

As she walked down the hallway toward the stairs, Nina heard Anderson's raised voice seeping from the solid door. She stopped, closed her eyes, and listened. The word bribery emerged for the second time in a week. She had never seen Anderson lose his temper with others. He only blew a fuse at her.

When her husband's voice calmed down, Nina flew up the stairs. Was Anderson going to use the money in the closet soon? How soon?

Heart racing, Nina sat on the edge of the bed and looked at herself in the mirror. She fiddled with a loose strand of hair. Hearing footsteps on the stairs, she rushed into the bathroom and locked herself in.

Anderson pounded on the door. "Catarina, don't take long. I need a shower."

Three bathrooms in the house, and he couldn't use another? "Just a minute." She turned on the sink faucet, ran her fingers under the hot water for a moment, and shut it off. Anderson's expression startled her when she opened the door. "Are you feeling well?"

"That stupid fish you made. It wasn't fresh." He brushed past her, pushing her aside.

What could she say in her defense? Nothing. Nothing she said would convince him she had bought the fish a few hours earlier from a reputable store. "I can get you some medicine."

Anderson looked at her for a few seconds and slammed the bathroom door in her face. Nina jumped and swallowed her anger. Worse than eating bad fish was swallowing Anderson's toxic behavior.

She grabbed her phone and opened her father's contact. Her fingers hesitated. She wanted to write to him about her escape, but what if Anderson saw the message? Nina wasn't supposed to have passwords on her phone or laptop. One of her husband's rules to control her. Early in their marriage, she learned not to leave anything important on her phone: no suspicious calls, no words with dual interpretations. Her contacts were limited to acquaintances from the country club and the services the couple used. Writing to her father would be risky. Maybe talking to him would be more prudent. She could go out now for a walk and call her dad, but Anderson would be suspicious. Nina jogged early in the morning. Never took walks in the evening.

The sound of the shower stopped. Minutes later, Anderson emerged from the bathroom in his bathrobe, drying his brown hair with a white towel. "I'm going out."

Nina glanced at him in the mirror's reflection. "An emergency at the hospital?"

He stopped drying his hair, squeezed the towel, and looked at her. "Snooping, huh? Don't you trust me?"

Wrong move, Nina, she scolded herself. "I was just making conversation."

"Not the time for small talk." He disappeared into the closet.

Another small miracle. Nina could call her father. She walked into her section of the closet and grabbed the nightgown. She took off the tight-fitting dress and let the light, fresh fabric slide down her skin. Her acting skill was improving. Maybe she should consider a gig in a community theater wherever she ended up after escaping her personal Alcatraz.

Dressed in a suit, he walked past her. "Don't wait for me. We'll save our date for tomorrow morning." He ran his fingers down her back.

Nina's skin prickled when his hand grazed her. His touch felt repugnant. Thinking that once she had melted in his arms, she shuddered. Anderson left the bedroom, and Nina counted his steps down the stairs. She waited when the garage door closed. After a while, she headed down to the study, a forbidden territory for her.

Sitting down on the armchair, she draped her legs over the leather arm. Her fingers touched the screen of her cell phone, and her father answered on the second ring.

"Nina, is everything alright?"

"I'm fine." How much was safe for him to know in case Anderson threatened him, demanding answers about Nina's disappearance?

"Nina, talk to me. I know something is going on. Did Anderson hurt you?"

Yes. He hurt me more than I can bear. The marks, though, go unseen. They are too deep. I have been bleeding for years, silently, alone. Nina took a deep breath. "Dad, listen carefully. I can't explain what's happening right now. It's complicated. Anderson hasn't laid a hand on me." She mentally laughed at her irony. "I agree with you—I can't go on like this. Please don't ask me questions. I will be okay. I'll stop by your house the night after tomorrow. Will you wait for me?"

A sigh came from the other end of the line. "Of course, I'll wait. And, Nina, if you need anything, anything, no matter how absurd it may seem, I'm here for you. Just ask."

Nina swallowed her tears. "I know, Dad. Please, forgive me."

"Forgive you for what?" He kept his voice low.

"For never taking your advice. For marrying Anderson despite your reservations. I was foolish, gullible, naïve."

"Sweetheart, don't apologize." His voice was filled with tenderness. "Don't blame yourself for what's going on, whatever it is. I just want you to know my love for you now is the same as the love I felt for my little girl with pigtails."

"I need to hang up. Love you, Dad." She covered her mouth to muffle a sob.

"I love you, my beautiful girl." Martin sighed.

Nina got up from the armchair and rubbed her damp eyes. She headed toward the door and turned back. Something at the foot of the heavy desk caught her attention. Bending down, she pulled out a piece of paper. She examined it. It was a kind of receipt. Nina didn't recognize the signature, but her eyes widened at the amount. In an act of courage and boldness, she folded the paper and ran back to her room. In the closet, she grabbed her handbag and opened the wallet. She slipped the folded receipt behind her driver's license.

Hearing a noise coming from the first floor, Nina turned off the lights and tucked herself under the soft covers. Anderson would expect her to be sleeping, and that was precisely what she would pretend to be doing. She squeezed her eyes shut and controlled her racing breath. Minutes later, her husband entered the room, turned on the closet light, not bothering to close the door, and left shortly after. Nina knew his routine. He would go to the bathroom and spend some time there, clipping his always short and clean nails, flossing and brushing his teeth and putting on one of his silk pajamas.

When Anderson pulled the covers and lay down, Nina heard him curse. She remained still, mimicking a soft snore. Anderson tossed and turned, shaking the mattress. A few minutes passed. He got up. Nina followed his silhouette in the bedroom with her half-closed eyes. Anderson opened the closet door, stepped inside, and then closed the door behind him. Nina saw light shining through the cracks, and her heart raced. What if he was taking the money? Agonizing minutes passed until Anderson came back to bed. Panic clawed at her chest.

CHAPTER 6

It's the big day, the most dangerous day of my life, Nina thought as she prepared breakfast for Anderson. She felt like she was riding a bicycle on a tightrope, with no safety net below. One wrong move, and Anderson would use all his twisted arsenal to make Nina suffer the consequences of betraying him.

Nina's hands trembled slightly and she noticed his gaze on them. "Are you feeling unwell?" Anderson looked at his wife with squinted eyes, like an eagle honing in on its prey. His question was far from being one of concern, Nina knew. While keeping his gaze fixed on her, he spread butter on his soft croissant.

The breakfast nook felt oppressive. Nina stood up from her seat across from Anderson. She filled a glass with freshly squeezed oranges for him. "It's the run this morning. I was feeling good and ran an extra block." Saying she should have eaten more would draw his attention to her waist with extra inches, hidden underneath the loose gym top.

But her shakiness had nothing to do with thirst or hunger.

The kettle whistled on the stovetop. Saved by the bell. Nina turned her back to Anderson and picked up the kettle. Slowly, she filled a mug with boiling water. Then she sat at the table with her mug, two saltine crackers, and a slice of low-fat cheese. Looking at the basket of golden, flaky croissants, Nina felt an uncontrollable urge to devour them, with plenty of butter and jam, and a rich and creamy cappuccino with the fattest milk she could find. The aroma of the croissants wafted into her nostrils and hit her brain, demanding the satisfaction of the craving. She imagined her mouth full of the rich, buttery taste of the flaky layers of the croissants. Bringing the cup to her lips, Nina wished the scent of chamomile could have the power to cleanse her nostrils of the addictive aromas surrounding her.

"I should get home earlier today." Anderson drank the rest of the orange juice.

Nina's heart raced. No. Her day was already timed. She would go to the country club, play tennis, have lunch with her friends, and then go to the salon. Nothing could go wrong. Nina needed the alibis for her plan. It had to seem like a normal day. "What time? I'll need to get dinner ready ahead of time."

"Are you monitoring my schedule?" Anderson stood up and looked at Nina with his eagle eyes.

"Not at all. It's roast beef with horseradish sauce day. I don't want it to come out dry."

Anderson walked down the hall, turning his back to Nina. "I don't care. Make it work." He threw his hand in the air.

Yes, I'll make it work. For me this time around. And tomorrow, you can have your coffee at the corner cafe or starve for all I care. She finished the rest of the crackers with low-fat cheese. She looked at the two croissants in the basket. No. Delayed gratification was a gift, a way to self-control until the right moment to savor the rewards.

Nina cleared the table and threw the croissants in the trash bin, just as Anderson expected her to do. Croissants had to be baked fresh daily. Well, not tomorrow.

After he left the house, Nina took a long shower. The tennis match was an hour away, enough time for her to organize the last details of the plan. Wearing a light blue pleated skirt and polo shirt, she went to the kitchen. She opened the pantry and grabbed the jars of horseradish paste. With a twisted sense of satisfaction, she poured the horseradish paste into the sink drain and turned the garburator on. The creamy white stream swirled like a serpent before disappearing with a gurgling sound. She smirked as she watched it vanish. The small pleasure felt great. *More to come tomorrow, Anderson.*

She left the house and tossed the jars in the neighbor's trash bin parked outside the garage, knowing they were away in Hawaii.

Back in her kitchen, Nina took the meat out of its packaging, seasoned it, and placed it in a covered baking dish to marinate.

Grabbing the vacuum cleaner, she tidied the living room, study, and hallway. She mopped the kitchen and powder room floors. At eleven o'clock, she left home for the country club. If Elisa and Giulia noticed anything different in Nina's attitude, they made no comments. The three women played two tennis matches, had lunch, and enjoyed the spa. Nina then left for her weekly meeting with Louis. The salon was full, but he took her to a chair near the storage door, where they had a little more privacy.

Louis draped the black cape over his client's shoulders and pinned up her hair. "Something's different about you."

"I guess." Nina looked at his image reflected in the mirror.

Louis frowned, his thick eyebrows meeting over his dark eyes. He took a comb and untangled small sections of Nina's hair. "A significant change."

How she wished she could tell him about her plan. Louis had been a good friend. But it wasn't prudent. "You'll know when the time comes, I promise."

Louis squeezed Nina's shoulder. "Don't do anything you'll regret."

"I only regret one thing: not doing anything."

He nodded, his face showing empathy. He gestured for Nina to go to the sink area. Perhaps sensing he wouldn't see Nina for a while, he took extra care in massaging her scalp. She closed her eyes and allowed her sore neck muscles to relax. The warm water cascaded over her hair in soothing streams. The fragrance of the shampoo enveloped her senses. Lavender and citrus mingled with the steam.

Nina had had so few pleasurable moments during her married years. Even small pleasures like a scalp massage had been overshadowed by the weight of Anderson's oppressive behavior. Could she imagine the joy of walking barefoot on the beach, feeling the warm sand and smelling the blooming flowers? Would she ever go back home, wherever this home would be, and feel peace even when the storms of life raged outside?

Nina dabbed the corner of the towel on her eyes. Even if she found out the money in the closet was gone, any scenario would be better than facing Anderson again. She longed for deep relationships with friends and a community, for deep or shallow conversations filled with laughter or tears of empathy. She longed for time well spent with her dad, talking about Mom and good times. Memories, making wonderful memories that would last throughout eternity. A legacy of respect, protection and love.

How much could she dream? Would God finally pick up the phone and answer her weak prayers?

With her hair now impeccably straight, Nina hugged her stylist. "Remember me."

"Always. Remember me if you need anything."

Nina paid the bill, leaving a generous tip, and headed home. Inside, she rushed upstairs.

In the walk-in closet, she slid her fingers along the cool drywall, her breath coming in shallow, quick bursts. She pushed open the panel, peering inside with a mixture of hope and fear. The portfolio folder was there. Her hands trembled as she touched inside the pocket. A rush of relief washed over her body. The money was there, and the bundle was thicker. She let out a laugh. Her heart pounded furiously as she got a pair of scissors from one of the drawers. She cut a small hole in the lining of her purse and hid the money. Folding the documents with Dutra's name and lines of other names and numbers, she slipped them inside.

Nina panicked when she heard a noise coming from downstairs. Anderson was home. She closed the hidden compartment. With one last, nervous glance around, she stashed the purse behind her winter jackets, turned off the light in the closet and shut the door. Forcing a calm expression on her face, she took a deep breath to steady herself.

The bedroom door swung open, and Anderson stormed in, the heavy oppression following him like a horrible shadow. "Haven't you started dinner yet?" He took off his white shirt and threw it on the bed.

"I prepped some things before leaving for the club." Nina's pulse pounded in her ears as she grabbed the shirt, her mind reeling with anxiety.

"I'll wait in the study." He grabbed a T-shirt from the closet, put it on, and left.

She breathed steadily. Rushing to the kitchen, she took the meat out of the refrigerator and placed it in the oven. She cleaned the asparagus and prepared the salad. Half an hour later, the smell of meat filled the air. Her mind raced ahead to her next move. Tonight, she was shifting the game. The charred remnants of the meat would be proof of that. Anderson would deal with a kitchen full of smoke. And Nina would be free.

She charged up the stairs, leaping two steps at a time. Opening the closet door, she grabbed her purse and yanked off her wedding ring and band. With trembling fingers, Nina hurled them into a shoe. The finality of the action ignited her resolve. She cast a glance at the bedroom. Her heart clenched at the sight of the bed—sleepless nights, tears, sex devoid of love.

Nina forced herself to move on, unwilling to linger in the past. She descended the stairs, breathing slowly. With her purse in hand, she knocked on the study door and cracked it open. "I'm going to the grocery store to get some horseradish."

Anderson looked at his wife, his gaze sparking with anger. From behind the massive desk, he looked like a judge. "You didn't know we ran out?"

"I'll be back in ten minutes."

He let out a grunt. Nina looked at the tall man with neatly cut brown hair, a surge of disgust flooding her chest.

Closing the door, she left the house, inhaling the polluted air of the city. A profound sense of freedom washed over her.

Nina walked down the sidewalk to the end of the street and flagged down a taxi.

Settling into the back seat of the car, she told the driver her destination. As the vehicle pulled away, she closed her eyes and rested her head against the seat, determined not to glance back.

The house that had been her prison for the past six years no longer deserved her last gaze.

CHAPTER 7

Martin flung open the front door and ran down the walkway that cut through the small front yard. Nina got out of the taxi and headed toward the gate. The porch lights glowed a soft, reassuring light, irradiating a sense of welcome. It was like coming back home; yet this wasn't Nina's last stop.

"What happened?" Martin embraced his daughter, stepped away and stared at her.

"Can we get inside?" She glanced around the street bathed in yellow streetlights.

In the living room, Nina dropped her bag on the couch, raced to her old room, and returned with the suitcase she pulled from the closet. Her father trailed behind her, his voice urgent as he asked her to explain what was going on. Nina sat on the couch, opened the suitcase, and took out a pair of jeans, a white T-shirt, the black hoodie, and the pair of sneakers. Stacking the clothes in her arms, she stood.

"I left home," she said.

"You left." His voice was a whisper. "Does Anderson know?"

"No. And if I take too long, he'll end up here." She looked nervously at the clock on the wall.

"What's your plan?" Anxiety crackled in Martin's voice. "I can find a safe place for you to stay. A women's shelter."

"Thanks, but I have everything planned." It was only a half-truth. The plan was to leave the city, catch the train, and escape as far away as possible. It didn't matter where to.

Martin ran a hand through his thinning hair. "You know you can count on me, right?"

She moved towards the hallway. "I know. I must get changed now." The ticking of the clock announced she was running out of time.

"I'll take you. We can drive anywhere." Concern laced Martin's thin face.

"I have to do this alone. For now, I don't want you to know where I'm going. Anderson will show up here sooner or later. He may threaten you."

Nina dashed to the bathroom before her father could argue. She changed clothes, feeling the roughness of the fabric, relieved to wear something that didn't pinch her waist and hips. Grabbing a black garbage bag from the vanity, she discarded her expensive dress pants and silk shirt, once symbols of her captivity. She threw away the shoes that was probably worth a month's salary for many. Slipping on the pair of inexpensive black sneakers, Nina tied the garbage bag and dropped it to the tiled floor.

She stared at her reflection in the mirror, and her eyes locked on the straightened hair that she loathed. Driven by a surge of defiance, she yanked the faucet handle, letting the water gush out. She leaned her head under the warm stream and ran her finger through her hair, washing away the sleek, artificial style.

Pulling a towel from the rod, Nina patted dry her hair, water dripping down her face and neck. Her natural curls sprung back to life like a withered plant revived by summer showers. Drying her face and neck, she grabbed a handful of paper tissues and wiped off her makeup.

She smiled at her reflection, a new face she was eager to rediscover. Catarina was giving way to Nina.

Back in the living room, she stood in front of her father, head high, curls bouncing. He brushed away a tear that streamed down his face. "Nina."

She kissed his cheek and sat on the sofa, pulling the black backpack from inside the suitcase. Nina swapped the contents from her designer purse into the backpack, tucking the money and documents away in a secure pocket inside it. "I left my phone at home." She stopped and rephrased the statement, "At Anderson's home. The battery is dead."

Martin disappeared down the hallway and soon returned with a box in hand. He motioned it to Nina. "Something told me you would need this."

Nina took the box and opened it. Inside was an inexpensive, pre-paid cell phone. Her eyes widened. "How did you know?"

Martin offered her a faint smile. "Call it coincidence. I call it divine revelation. I always pray for you, Nina, for your protection and safety."

He'd prayed for her. The realization struck Nina with a gentle force. Martin had never lost his faith, not even when her mother died. Nina's faith had corroded as the months under Anderson's oppressive rule dragged on. His tyranny chipped away at her hope, leaving her spirit weary and dry, like the bones in the desert the Bible talked about.

As Nina looked at her father, the emotions mingled with a faint hope that life could be better. But before she could heal, Nina had to confront her ghosts. Those shadows of fear and pain had clung to her for so long. It wasn't just about taking a train somewhere and moving on; it was about braving storms before the dawning of a new day.

She wanted Nina back. But she hardly knew herself anymore. That Nina lay underneath layers of self-doubt. Her job was to unearth her essence, like an archeologist digging through layers of the past, to uncover fragments of what was still preserved. Dared she say it was the identity God had engraved in her soul? Would her faith be strong enough to surrender the job of unearthing her essence to him?

"Continue praying for me, Dad." The tears she had been holding back spilled over.

Martin wrapped his slender arms around her shoulders. "Always. I'll always be with you. Always cover you in prayer, my dear Nina."

She brushed away the tears with her thumb, nodded and kissed him. With a long sigh, she tossed the cellphone in the backpack. Zipping up the dark suitcase, Nina stood up and set it on its wheels. Her father pulled an envelope from his pants pocket and handed it to her.

"It's not much, but it should help you some," he said.

Nina opened the envelope and pulled out some bills. It didn't seem right to take money from her father when she had a small fortune in her backpack. But explaining the origin of the money she carried would take time, which was scarce at that moment. She tucked the envelope into her backpack. "Thank you. I'll pay you back once I find a job." With little work experience, the best Nina could only hope to find was a part-time job in a cafe or a store. She would think about it later when she settled somewhere.

Embracing her father with all the strength her arms could muster, Nina whispered everything would be alright. Yet she knew a tremendous challenge loomed ahead like a storm. Six years of captivity had stripped her of the skills to fend for herself. Her heart thumped at the thought of soon arriving at the bustling train station, engulfed by a surge of people flowing in and out of the cars. When was the last time Nina had ridden in public transit? Six years ago.

The die was cast. Nina slid into the taxi as she clutched the suitcase and the backpack beside her. A mix of fear and determination swirled within her. As the taxi pulled away, a wave of adrenaline surged through her, cementing the realization that there was no turning back. Waving goodbye to her father, Nina grappled with the enormity of her decision. The vehicle rounded the corner and glided down the street under a moonless sky. Once again, Nina rested her head against the seat and watched her old neighborhood vanish in the rearview mirror.

Freedom and uncertainty awaited her.

As the taxi cruised through the light traffic of late evening, Nina thought of Anderson. He would have realized by now she was gone, meat burning in the oven and the smoke alarm blaring. He would be cursing her through gritted teeth while calling 911.

Nina would buy time until everything settled at home. She dared pray she would be miles away by the time Anderson showed up at her father's house, demanding answers about his wife's whereabouts. He would fume when he learned Nina was long gone.

The swaying of the taxi through traffic made Nina more anxious. It felt as if she was slipping through a portal into a new world. She hoped the characters in this new story would be warmer and more genuine. Nina was tired of Giulia and Eliana, of Milena and Solos. She didn't expect perfection from people; far from it, as everybody had their own secrets, sins, and pains. What she hoped for was to embrace her true self—Nina with messy hair, someone who made foolish decisions but genuinely wanted to do the right thing. Perhaps in this new dimension, she could cry when she was sad or felt pain. Perhaps she could allow herself to laugh, count the stars, and hum for no reason. She hoped that the new characters of these chapters would be flesh and blood, not plastic, like shop mannequins.

The taxi stopped, and Nina opened her eyes. The enormous train station was right next to her, with hurried passengers rushing along the sidewalk. Nina paid for the ride and stepped out, dragging the suitcase behind her, the crowd swallowing the solitary passenger. She fell into the flow of rushing people, searching for signs that would guide her to where she could buy a ticket. Where would she go? Far away wasn't an actual destination.

As she searched for the ticket sales booth, Nina realized that almost everything was automated. Her heart raced once again with the question: Where would she go? She joined one line of passengers and watched as they bought tickets and found their way to the platforms. A young man in a leather jacket in front of her was next, and Nina peeked over his shoulder, trying to understand the mystery of the machine that spat out tickets. To her relief, she could use cash. When her turn came, Nina pressed the buttons randomly. She bought the most expensive ticket, hoping it would take her far away. With the ticket in hand, she looked for her platform, already feeling dizzy with the crowd and the surrounding noise.

Only when she was inside the train, her suitcase tucked underneath her legs and the backpack nestled securely beside her, did Nina allow herself to relax a bit. The train moved, leaving the city behind. Nina rested her head against the window glass, relieved that the worst was over. She was free from Anderson, from the life full of traps, from the control, the humiliation, and the pain.

As the train raced through the dark landscape, everything became a blur. Nina's mind raced back to a movie she'd seen years ago. A weary and disillusioned businessman boarded a train after work and dozed off. When he awoke, the world outside had transformed and looked like a page from a history book. Gas lamps flickered, passengers in tailored suits and dresses bustled about. Confused, the passenger asked the ticket agent where they were. The bald man in a vintage uniform replied that this was the last stop of the man's life, and he should savor it before it was over.

Nina had given little thought to the profound meaning of the movie at the time. But now, as the train roared on, it dawned on her—she needed to embrace this moment, this new chapter, as if her last.

What would the morning sun unveil to her?

CHAPTER 8

The train's gradual deceleration woke Nina from a deep sleep. How long had she been asleep? Rubbing her dry, sticky lips, she pulled her cell phone out of the jacket pocket. Eight hours—she had slept for eight uninterrupted hours. Nina couldn't remember the last time she had slept that long. Perhaps when Anderson was traveling, giving her some peace; he would call from wherever he was, no matter the time zone, to check on her. That was the excuse he'd give, but it was really to keep tabs on her life.

Nina looked out the window, the platform coming into view like a scene in slow motion. Sleepy passengers waited outside, some distracted by their phones or books, some holding large suitcases, others just a backpack or a briefcase.

The world outside awoke with the soft glow of the rising sun. It bathed the trees and houses that ran by Nina's window, painting them in pastel hues. The train stopped smoothly as if respecting the tired travelers who had spent hours sitting on uncomfortable seats. Nina picked up the backpack from the seat beside her, straps secured around her wrist. Her car was almost empty. This was Nina's first stop. She planned to travel further east. Not that it mattered, as long as she stayed far away from Anderson: north, south, east, west, but far, very far.

The electronic voice over the loudspeaker announced the name of the station and the city, adding that the stop would last ten minutes. Nina stood up and stretched her sore legs and arms to get the circulation going. Her right hand was numb. Bending down, she placed the suitcase upright and pulled the handle. She grabbed the backpack and threw it over her shoulder. Nina waited for a passenger to pass with her sleeping child, who had his head drooped over the young woman's shoulder. Dragging the suitcase along the aisle, she got off onto the platform.

She looked around, feeling her curly hair with her fingers, reading the signs and electronic schedule. She moved towards the signs showing the ticket counters. This station was much smaller than the previous one, but the hallways were long, resembling a maze. Nina pulled her suitcase, the wheels making a rhythmic noise as they rolled over the tiled floor. She found the counter and considered her destination options. The line behind her grew, and she made a quick decision under the pressure. The next train would leave in an hour, plenty of time for her to recover from the first leg of the long journey.

Nina had never heard of the city name printed on the ticket. It was probably for the best—Anderson wouldn't know it either. Later, she planned to look it up online to get acquainted with the area and start searching for a job and a place to stay.

When she turned right down a long corridor, a tantalizing aroma entered her nostrils, making her mouth water. She was hungry. Her last meal had been twenty hours earlier, and she had eaten a small portion.

A cafe caught Nina's attention. The glass case below the counter displayed breads, pastries, and croissants. The aroma of coffee wafted through the air. Nina stopped by the counter, and a barista with two long braids cascading down her shoulder greeted her.

"What can I get ya?" she asked.

Nina looked at the display case and then back at the young woman. "Two croissants, a piece of chocolate cake, and a large cappuccino to go." Her stomach gurgled.

The barista tapped the cash register, received Nina's money, and turned to the coffee machine. It came to life, sputtering the steaming, aromatic coffee, inviting other patrons to come closer. Minutes later, Nina was devouring the croissants and the decadent slice of cake by the counter. She indulged in the flaky and gooey textures of the pastries, licking her lips and fingers.

Other customers arrived, ordering their breakfast. Satisfied, Nina wiped her mouth and grabbed the disposable coffee cup, thanking the barista and wishing her a good day. The sugar and caffeine worked wonders for Nina's spirits. She was now prepared and fueled up for the next leg of the journey toward freedom.

She stopped near the women's restroom and called her father, who let out a sigh of relief. No, Anderson hadn't contacted him to check on Catarina. She found it peculiar that he showed no interest, and her apprehension threatened to return. What if he had hired a detective to look for her? No one knew about her trip and where she had gone, but detectives would find a way to discover. It was their job to track people down like hounds tracking foxes.

"I'm fine, Dad," she said, her voice cheerful. "As soon as I settle down, I'll let you know where."

"Let me know if you need me. Please."

"I promise. I'm okay. Really." The sounds of passengers' voices echoed around Nina.

They said their goodbyes, Nina assuring her father she'd call often. Her simple cell phone was a blessing, a line just between her and her father. The one she tossed somewhere in the closet had advanced technology but subjected her to relentless surveillance.

Nina walked into the restroom and looked at herself in the mirror that stretched along the counter with several sinks. Her curly hair, hastily arranged the night before, was flattened on one side and tangled on the other. The reflection that stared back at her from the mirror was not the woman her arrogant husband had shaped. Instead, she saw Nina, a woman in a shell of fear, eager to break free. How long would that process take?

A plump woman with graying hair and short, uneven bangs appeared in the reflection beside Nina. Creases of countless smiles around her mouth softened her weathered face. When she smiled, the wrinkles around her eyes deepened, giving her an expression of warmth and wisdom. Nina mirrored her smile.

"Long trip?" the woman asked, combing her chin-length hair with pudgy finger.

"One more leg to go." Nina moved away from the sink, but the woman shifted her heavy bag on her shoulder and faced the young woman.

"Where are you off to?"

Just traveler talk, don't worry. Nina tried to convince herself that the woman was not a detective sent by Anderson. "East." Vague enough information.

The woman studied Nina's face. "Going wherever the heart takes you, huh?"

Nina felt uneasy. "Something like that."

"Those are the best places. Safe travels." The woman turned and exited the restroom, the large bag weighing on her shoulder.

Nina rushed into a stall and locked the door. She leaned the suitcase against the door and controlled her rapid breathing. After using the toilet, Nina opened the door and peeked around. Two young women were washing their hands and chatting. Nina washed her hands and soon exited into the long corridor of the station. The loudspeaker announced her train. She took the ticket from the pocket of her hoodie and checked the platform number again: four.

Pulling her suitcase, she looked at the signs and followed the arrows. The sound of wheels on the tracks grew louder. Nina glanced at the digital display with the train schedules and platform numbers and quickened her pace. As she walked down the corridor, it stretched out before her like an endless maze of reflections in infinite mirrors. Nina ran, her suitcase tipping over from time to time. She hurried past several passengers.

Her eyes darted from one end of the maze of hallways to the other. Each one seemed to twist and turn unpredictably, electronic boards flashing messages and numbers. Her vision blurred. The numbers made no sense. A train departed from the platform in front of her, and another arrived, the metallic screeches of the wheels blending with the murmur of conversations. The loudspeaker made a last call for passengers heading to the same destination as Nina. She turned around, but couldn't locate her platform. The signs appeared to have multiplied. Nina approached a man waiting for the train and asked about platform four.

"Oh, it's on the other side." He pointed with his long finger to the opposite platform, past the train tracks.

Nina ran off without even thanking him. She shot down the hallway like a bullet, zigzagging around passengers and janitors with their large service carts. When she turned the corner toward platform four, she halted. The train was leaving, sliding smoothly along the tracks. A man bumped into her, apologized, and continued his way. Nina moved away from the center of the corridor and leaned against the wall. She lowered her head and ran her fingers over the sweaty forehead. She jumped when she felt someone poking her shoulder.

"Looks like you missed your train." It was the plump woman from the restroom.

Nina looked at the woman, nodding in defeat. "This place is a maze." Disheartened, she let her head droop. She would have to find her way back to the ticket counters.

The woman stayed by Nina's side. *Doesn't she have to take the train? Why is she still here?* The woman's wrinkled hands opened her large bag and disappeared inside. Soon, her fingers returned with two tickets. "If your intention is to follow your heart on this journey, I have a suggestion: come with me."

Nina almost laughed. She would be crazy to follow a stranger to a strange place. Still, Nina had no clear destination in mind. It didn't matter much where she ended up. She was already far away from Anderson. If she didn't like the place, she could go to another. No one would keep her where she didn't want to stay. Not anymore.

"I know it seems like a strange invitation, but something tells me you will like Grace Harbor." The woman smiled, her eyes shining.

Nina scrutinized the woman's face, looking for any clues that might suggest a cause for concern. Perhaps signs of madness. Nina had not been good at assessing people's intentions, as evidenced by the fact she had married Anderson. However, the woman's gaze expressed something authentic, a kind of candor or innocence. Or else she deserved an Oscar.

The loudspeaker announced the train to Grace Harbor. The woman waved the tickets and pointed to the platform. "That's our train." Her voice had a sing-song cadence.

Nina found herself following the woman, who walked ahead, the large bag bouncing on her back. The train glided along the tracks and came to a stop.

"Grace Harbor, passengers to Grace Harbor. Proceed to platform four," the mechanical voice announced.

Nina jumped. Platform four? How was that possible? Hadn't she gotten lost in the maze of hallways in search of the same number and ended up missing the train? How was she now right back at the same platform? Anxiety coursed beneath her skin like creeping critters.

The train door slid open. Some passengers exited, and a few got on. The woman turned to Nina and gestured for her to hurry. At the door, Nina hesitated. Everything felt too surreal to risk moving forward, just like the passenger in that movie she had seen. Where would she end up?

Nina considered backing away and stopped. A man bumped into her, sending her to the ground. The lady came over and pulled her by the arm. Nina soon found herself on the aisle of the train.

"Sit down, sit down. Are you hurt?" Nina's travel companion asked.

Nina took her seat and shook her head. "I'm fine. Where's my suitcase?" She clutched the backpack nervously.

The woman pointed to the seat beside her. "Safe and sound." She placed the suitcase under the front seat and sat down.

The train gave a slight jerk and started moving. Nina looked out the window and focused on the huge number four flashing on the electronic display. That was a Twilight Zone-worthy moment.

The loudspeaker chimed:

"Next stops, Mapleton and Grace Harbor."

Nina sank into the vinyl seat, muscles burning. Her thoughts drifted to the name Grace Harbor. Would it be a place of renewal and new beginnings? The train chugged forward, leaving the city. Nina's heart filled with anticipation of what this journey—and Grace Harbor—might hold.

CHAPTER 9

"By the way, my name is Grace," the woman said, her voice carrying a gentle warmth as she extended her hand toward Nina, her smile soft and inviting.

"Grace?" Nina took the woman's warm hand and shook it.

"Just a coincidence," Grace replied with a twinkle in her eye. "I'm Grace from Grace Harbor—unforgettable, isn't it?"

"Indeed." The coincidences unsettled Nina. First, her encounter with Grace in the restroom. Then, her getting lost in the train station and the free tickets. Now, the woman's name. "What kind of place is Grace Harbor? I figure it's by the sea."

The train's gentle sway continued. The indistinct noises of the few passengers blended with the click-clack of the wheels.

Grace settled back in the seat and placed her bag on the floor. "It's quaint. Few residents in the winter, but thousands more in the summer. With the off-season starting, things are quieter now."

Nina glanced out the window, the golden wheat fields stretching endlessly toward the horizon. No skyscrapers, highways—just open fields and the sky with fluffy clouds. She looked back at Grace. "How far is Grace Harbor?"

"A three-hour ride. Mapleton is halfway. We can stop there to grab a bite."

Nina's stomach growled, craving something more substantial after the empty calories she'd consumed earlier. "Sounds good." She turned her gaze to the bald head in front of her. Whose ticket had Grace given to her? Nina was curious, but the more questions she asked, the more she'd have to answer. Grace's next words surprised her:

"The ticket was for my niece. I came to settle some family matters with my sister. We thought it'd be best for Hannah to stay with me. But she backed out at the last minute." Grace pursed her lips in a slight frown. "Young people can be stubborn. They think they can solve any problems without understanding the realities of life."

Nina nodded. That was a truth she knew well. If she hadn't been so stubborn, she wouldn't be fleeing from her husband. Ex-husband. Husband. There had been no divorce, just—Anderson would use this against her—abandonment.

And theft.

Nina clutched the backpack. "True."

Her eyelids grew heavy. She closed them, letting the rhythmic clatter of the train on the tracks lull her to sleep. Her final thoughts were of her farewell to her father. She would miss him. Perhaps someday he could visit her in Grace Harbor or wherever she might end up if she didn't adapt to the coastal town.

***

Nina jolted awake, grumbling as she felt firm fingers on her shoulder. She opened her eyes to find Grace standing beside her.

"We only have ten minutes at the stop. Let's grab a snack."

Nina glanced at her suitcase under the seat and bent to retrieve it. Grace shook her head, indicating that the man in front would watch it. Grace trusted a stranger too much. Then again, Nina's new Walmart wardrobe wasn't exactly a treasure. The backpack was important.

They disembarked on the platform, greeted by a sign: Welcome to Mapleton. The station was small, devoid of maze-like corridors. The convenience store was just a few steps away. Nina ordered a coffee and a hefty three-layered sandwich of white bread, deli meats, cheese, and tomato, with a drippy white sauce. Grace chose a cup of soup-to-go and two bananas.

As the loudspeaker announced the train's departure, Nina was already devouring her lunch beside Grace on the train. She licked her fingers, savoring every drop of sauce and crumb of bread.

"I brought an extra banana if you want." Grace took another spoonful of soup.

She must think I'm a glutton. If only she knew. "Maybe later."

The journey continued, with the fields giving way to trees dressed in vibrant oranges and reds. The explosion of colors was a feast for Nina's eyes, so often accustomed to the drab sophistication of city life. Her excitement wasn't solely from the caffeine, but from the anticipation of Grace Harbor. The name sounded serene. Grace's description painted it as a picturesque place, perhaps with charming houses, white fences, and window boxes overflowing with flowers. There would be a quaint main street with charming shops and friendly faces, like a peaceful oil painting. Nina chuckled, and Grace looked at her with curiosity. Her imagination was running wild. Coincidences rarely happened, and Nina's quota had already been exceeded in the past twelve hours.

Grace nudged Nina and handed her the banana. They peeled their fruit while gazing out the window. The landscape of yellows and reds continued for half an hour before the first houses cropped up.

"What kind of accommodation would you prefer, dear?" Grace folded banana peel and tossed it back into the paper bag.

That was a good question. Surely Grace Harbor had inns or B&B's. "Could you recommend a clean and affordable place?"

"I know the perfect spot: Tranquility-by-the-Sea."

Nina found the name amusing. Tranquility-by-the-Sea. Had she stepped into a fairy tale where everything seemed perfect? Perhaps the locals lived in a fantasy, deluding themselves about life's harsh realities. "Is it expensive?"

Grace looked at Nina. "Even if it were, you'd get a special rate."

Too much kindness and charity. It didn't seem quite right. "I'd prefer to stay somewhere at a fair price." Her tone was harsher than she intended.

Grace turned her gaze to the scenery before returning to Nina. "Those blessed much find it in their hearts to give much."

Nina didn't understand the comment. Perhaps Tranquility-by-the-Sea was Grace's home, and she was simply trying to help a fellow traveler. "I was rude. I apologize."

Grace nodded. "Tranquility-by-the-Sea is an inn run by dear friends. It's cozy, clean, and affordable. Esther and Parker Baek are generous people."

Nina assumed Esther and Parker were an elderly couple like Grace. "I'd like to see the inn."

"That will be our first stop when we get off the train." The sing-song cadence returned.

As if on cue, the electronic voice announced,

"Next stop, Grace Harbor."

The passengers gathered their belongings. Nina pulled her suitcase upright. Her excitement surged again as she saw the platform that seemed straight out of a historical novel. Outside, the station radiated charm, with brick walls softened by ivy and flowering vines. A rustic wooden sign displayed the name of the town: Grace Harbor. Despite the autumn chill, flowerpots hung from the broad columns. Ahead, Nina could see a tranquil street divided by a line of trees with autumn leaves.

The train came to a stop, and the passengers moved towards the door. Grace gestured for Nina to go ahead. The sea breeze hinted at the ocean's proximity, mingling with the sweet scent of early autumn.

"Can you manage two blocks with your suitcase?" Grace adjusted the strap of the large bag, but seemed not to be bothered by its bulkiness.

"Of course. I'll manage with the wheels." A burst of energy surged through Nina's tired body. She pulled her suitcase along the wide sidewalk, surprised by Grace's popularity, as the passers-by greeted her. "Are you some kind of local celebrity? The mayor?" Nina struggled to keep up with Grace's brisk pace.

The older woman waved at a man walking his dog and laughed. "Neither a celebrity nor the mayor. Just an ordinary citizen."

Nina doubted Grace was an ordinary citizen. Ordinary people existed in their little bubbles of family, work and mundane duties. People didn't recognize and greet them enthusiastically in the streets like they did with Grace.

After walking two blocks and making several stops for Grace to chat with locals, they arrived at a white two-story house with sea blue windows. A white gazebo took center stage in the yard, adorned with fishing ropes and an anchor. The flower beds still thrived despite the threats of the cooler evenings. Nina dragged her suitcase along the stone pathway, following Grace to the sea blue door. Grace turned the doorknob and stepped inside. Nina's eyes widened as she entered the reception area, not for its opulence, but for its charming and cozy atmosphere. The décor was in soothing pastel blues and whites, as if the coastal environment outside had invaded the house.

Grace approached the white counter and rang the bell. A feminine voice announced she was coming, followed by a younger voice repeating the phrase.

"Esther and Jade Baek," Grace explained to Nina.

A tall woman with Asian features stepped out from a white side door, followed by a short, smiling girl with pigtails around ten years old.

Nina looked at the girl, studying her face. She resembled the tall woman, but had distinct features of Down syndrome.

The girl stepped in front of the woman and opened the guest book on the counter. "Hi, Auntie Grace. Who's your friend? Is she staying here at Tranquility-by-the-Sea?"

"This is Nina," Grace introduced her traveling companion. "Do you have a room for her?"

"Nice to meet you," the girl said, extending her small hand. "I'm Jade, and this is my mother, Esther. We do have rooms available."

"The pleasure is mine, Jade." Nina shook the girl's hand and then greeted Esther. "I'm not sure how long I'll be staying."

Jade picked up a pen and turned the book toward Nina. "Write your full name and address." She smiled with an air of importance.

Full name? Adams. But address? Nina hadn't considered she'd need to provide personal information. Of course, any hotel or inn would require those details. She took Jade's pen and looked at the list of names in the book.

Grace took the pen from Nina's hand and wrote something on the line Jade indicated. "For now, she can use my address."

Esther looked from Grace to Nina. "Of course, no problem."

"Why does she need to stay here if she lives with you?" Jade asked, her brown eyes glistening with curiosity.

Grace set aside the pen after writing the address and smiled at Jade. "She doesn't live with me. I'm her reference."

Jade glanced at her mother, who gave a subtle signal for the girl to stay quiet. Nina sighed in relief. She needed smart strategies to avoid dangerous questions. Taking back the pen, she wrote her name: Nina Adams. She paid for her first week's stay in cash, afraid that would raise suspicion. Neither woman said anything, but Jade looked at the money with interest.

"Our traveler must be tired," Grace said. "Jade, why don't you show Nina to her room?"

"Okay. Let's go." Jade stepped out from behind the counter and crossed the foyer toward the white-railed staircase.

Nina picked up her suitcase and turned to Grace. "Thank you."

"'Those blessed much find it in their hearts to give much.' I hope you have a wonderful stay," Grace replied with a smile.

Nina followed Jade up the stairs, guessing that Grace would discuss her unexpected arrival with Esther.

Fatigue overtook Nina. The initial excitement had turned into exhaustion. Her nerves were on edge, and adrenaline coursed wildly through her body. The distance she had put between herself and Anderson was significant, but the fear of being found had grown. Perhaps he didn't care about what happened to his wife, but he would certainly search for her when he discovered the missing money and documents.

Jade crossed the carpeted hallway and opened the last door. "This is your room. It's pretty."

Nina pulled in her suitcase and entered the room. If the town seemed like something out of a fairy tale, the room was like a scene from an enchanted story. The white wrought-iron bed was covered with a pure white crocheted bedspread. Several white pillows with frilly cases adorned the bed. The wallpaper was striped in white and blue, bringing a touch of the sea indoors. An antique white dresser shared space with a pastel blue desk. The window was cracked open, and Nina could see the sea beyond. "It's really pretty, Jade."

"I painted that." The girl pointed to a framed watercolor picture of the sea with seagulls and a kite.

Nina moved closer to the painting. "It's beautiful. Is it from the beach out front?"

Jade cocked her head, making her pigtails sway. "Yes. Parker likes to fish off the pier."

Parker. Nina struggled to remember who Parker was. Grace had mentioned that he and Esther were the owners of the inn. Esther wasn't elderly, though. "It must be a lovely beach."

"Want to go there now?" Jade's eyes sparkled with excitement.

"Now I need a bath and some rest."

A voice from the hallway, which Nina recognized as Esther's, called out to Jade. The girl made a funny face. "My mom thinks I talk too much. If you want to see the beach, tell me."

"Thank you. I'd like that." Nina pointed to the painting. "You're very talented."

"Jade," the voice called out with more emphasis.

The girl scrunched her nose. "Coming, Mom." She turned back to Nina. "I can also teach you to paint."

"Deal." Nina smiled and waved at Jade as she ran down the hallway.

Turning around the room, Nina examined every piece of furniture and details of the serene ambiance. Tranquility-by-the-Sea lived up to its name. Nina fervently wished she could find that same tranquility in her troubled soul. A painful chapter of her life was ending, and others would begin. She was hopeful.

She was afraid.

CHAPTER 10

The narrow strip of sea visible from Nina's window was partially obscured by neighboring houses, yet the salty air reached her room with vibrant intensity. She stole another glance at the view outside before closing the window. Opening the suitcase on the bed, Nina unpacked her new clothes, neatly storing them in the small closet. She tossed her underwear into the dresser drawer and carried her toiletries to the small, clean bathroom.

Calling her father, Nina reassured him she had settled in and felt secure. That was all Martin Adams needed to know. Anderson had not contacted him. What might be happening at the house? Was Anderson taking his time to plot revenge? The questions gnawed at Nina's mind like relentless pests in an abandoned garden. She didn't want to look over her shoulder anxiously, but peace hadn't accompanied her on this trip.

She retrieved her backpack, pulling out the money and the document. She needed to open a bank account if she stayed in Grace Harbor. The money was a constant reminder that Anderson would not rest until he reclaimed it. How long before he realized it was missing?

Putting the bundle of money in the envelope, she tucked it at the bottom of a drawer and placed her father's money into her wallet. She selected a clean outfit, laid it on the bed, and headed to the bathroom. The small shower was nothing like the fancy marble one she'd had before, but she could have some privacy and take a shower without Anderson bothering her. He always interrupted her moments of comfort with his incessant needs.

Nina stood under the warm water, planning her next moves, knowing that each step she took in Grace Harbor would tie her more to the town. First, she would go to the bank. Then she'd start job hunting. She would explore the town and inquire about job openings, even if it meant waiting tables. With her limited experience, her options were slim.

Wrapping herself in a soft, fresh towel, she returned to the room and got dressed in dark jeans and a gray sweater. Her wardrobe was minimal, but comfortable. She applied a generous layer of leave-in conditioner to her hair, shaping the curls. She skipped the makeup, wanting to see her true self in the mirror.

Her stomach reminded Nina it was suppertime. She grabbed the hoodie and backpack, locked the room and went down to the reception area. No one was there. Nina walked to a cozy nook, where a bookshelf lined one wall, and a large window overlooked the sidewalk and the tree-lined street. Three armchairs were arranged around a coffee table, and in the corner, facing the window, was a large, shell-shaped chair with plush upholstery—a perfect spot for reading and reflecting.

"Nina," Esther appeared in the doorway. "Do you need anything?"

"Hi, I was wondering where I can get supper. Nothing fancy."

"We only serve breakfast, but there are several bistros on Main Street. I recommend Beth's. She serves homemade meals."

"What's the name of the bistro?"

"Beth's Bistro." Esther laughed. "You can't miss it."

Nina thanked her. The woman wore a red sweater that highlighted her distinctive traits. How much had she endured, caring for a special needs child? Nina knew little about it, despite having once considered social work, a dream that had faded. A country club acquaintance had a son with autism, kept away from prying eyes in a society where appearances mattered. Jade seemed well-adjusted, and certainly her mother treated her with love and care. "Jade mentioned she'd like to show me the beach. Is it all right if we go for a walk later?"

Esther nodded. "She'd love that. She enjoys being a guide for guests. If you can endure her chatter, feel free. I won't tell her now, or she might skip supper in excitement. Ask her when you come back. We live in the cottage just behind the inn." Esther pointed to the window. "You can't miss it."

Nina craned her neck and squinted. "I can't really see it."

"The spruces give us privacy. Just follow the stone pathway and stop by when you come back."

"Of course. And thanks for the tips. I'll head out now and talk to Jade soon."

Nina stepped outside, inhaling the salty air. She walked two blocks and found Beth's Bistro next to a charming little shop, Love at Second Sight. Nina crossed the street, drawn to the shop's window display. Antique decor items were neatly arranged alongside mannequins dressed in vintage clothing. At the back of the shop, she spotted a cozy corner with a couch and a bookcase. That place would be worth visiting the next day. Nina hoped they wanted help.

Turning her attention back to the rumbling stomach, Nina entered the bistro. A wonderful aroma greeted her, confirming that Esther's recommendation was spot-on. A young server approached Nina, her apron full of crayons.

"Welcome to Beth's Bistro. Will you be dining in or taking out?"

"I'll dine in." Nina looked around, doubtful the server would find a seat for her. Patrons of different ages occupied the few tables, some showing interest in the newcomer. Some even waved at her.

The smiling server approached a table where an elderly couple was finishing their soup. She whispered something to them, and they nodded. Turning to Nina, she said,

"You can share Nelson and Celia's table." She headed toward the kitchen.

Nina found it odd to sit with the elderly couple, but complied. Her stomach was impatient.

"Good evening, young lady," the man with thick-framed glasses said. "Just passing through our charming village?"

His wife lightly tapped his arm. "Grace Harbor is not a village. It's a town."

The man chuckled. "What difference does it make? We are small enough to be called a village, where everybody knows everybody. It might seem like a bad thing, but it's a good thing."

Nina smiled awkwardly. The woman set her spoon down and leaned over the table, peering through her old-fashioned glasses. "How long have you been in our town?" She emphasized the last word.

"Just got here." Was everybody in Grace Harbor that curious? Things could be complicated if they were. Nina wasn't ready to answer questions about her life and the reason for her stay.

"How wonderful! I hope you love it and stay for a long time."

The man sighed. "Leave the young lady alone."

"I'm just trying to be polite." Celia pursed her thin lips.

Nina hoped the elderly couple's argument would keep them from asking her more questions. The server returned with the couple's bill. The man took money from his wallet and handed it to the server.

"I'll get the change," she said.

Nelson stood and waved his hand. "No, no. Use the change to pay for her meal." He smiled and gestured towards Nina.

"Oh, no, please." Nina shook her head.

Celia also stood. "Take it as a warm welcome to our town."

Nina looked at the couple, wide-eyed. "I don't know what to say."

"You don't need to say anything. Enjoy your meal." Nelson offered his arm to Celia, waved goodbye to Nina and the server, and left.

Nina looked at the server. "I'm speechless."

The young woman collected the dirty plates, stacking them on her arm. "Nelson and Celia are like that. After losing their son to cancer, they found that generosity made them feel better. Nelson was known as the town's Scrooge back then." She laughed. "By the way, I'm Simone." She pointed to the nameplate on her yellow shirt.

"Nina." She accepted the menu Simone handed her. "What a story!"

After placing her order, Nina nibbled on the fresh bread Simone brought to the table and observed the bistro's patrons. Some chatted and laughed, while others talked with serious expressions. How many of them were passing through, like Nina, and how many called Grace Harbor home? She had arrived only hours earlier, but felt a deep curiosity about the people. Esther and her special daughter, Jade. Grace, with her local popularity. Simone, who seemed to know her customers well. Celia and Nelson, with their story of loss.

Nina had lived six years cocooned in an artificial world, hearing gossip, rumors, and lies from Guilia, Eliana and her own husband. Perhaps the most genuine person was Milena, Dutra's young wife. In a few hours, she had spoken more truths than anyone Nina had known in her years of marriage.

Simone brought the food on a tray and set the dishes before Nina: salad, soup, beef stew with mashed potatoes, and more bread. Without the constraints of portions, calories, and nutrients, without Anderson overseeing every bite she took, Nina ate slowly, savoring the flavors. Half an hour later, her plates were empty and her stomach full. She ordered a slice of apple pie and a strong coffee. Nina wondered if the money Nelson had left to cover her bill would be enough. Simone assured her it was, and that she had even received a generous tip.

Nina said goodbye to the friendly server and stepped onto the sidewalk, walking by Love at Second Sight once more. Through the shop window, she saw four women seated in the corner where the bookshelf was, each with a book. Could it be a book club? Nina was intrigued, but it was getting late for her walk with Jade. She would ask Esther about the shop later.

Back at Tranquility, Nina circled the two-story building and reached the cottage nestled behind a line of spruces. The exterior had a wraparound porch with a wooden swing. The white shutters allowed soft light to filter through.

She knocked on the rustic door, and Jade opened it as if she had been waiting.

"Hi, Nina. Can we go for a walk now?" The girl was wearing a pair of unicorn-patterned leggings and a cream sweater. Her sneakers had golden laces.

"I'm ready and curious to see the beach. Let your mom know we're leaving." Nina inhaled the crisp evening air, thinking how much she'd missed in life.

Esther crossed the cozy living room toward the door, drying her hands with a dish towel. "Hi, Nina. Enjoy your walk."

"Thank you."

"Let's go." Jade took Nina's hand.

Feeling the small, soft hand in hers, Nina was filled with a special fondness for the girl. She was reminded of the times she used to walk hand in hand with her mother in what now seemed like a distant dream. Her mother had been a kind and patient woman who loved taking her daughter out for ice cream around the neighborhood. Simple joys of times long gone, interrupted by Tanya's premature death after an appendectomy.

Nina and Jade crossed the street and continued towards the beach. She wondered why Esther had allowed her daughter to go out with a stranger, but considering what she had already learned about Grace Harbor and its residents, she recognized the strong sense of community.

They strolled past the charming houses lining the streets. The soothing sounds of the waves mingled with the salty breeze.

"Do you know what Jade means?" The girl looked up at Nina.

"A precious stone?"

Jade nodded. "My mother said I'm her precious stone. That's why I got this name."

"It's beautiful. Your mother is right."

Jade tightened her grip on Nina's hand as they reached the beach. "What does your name mean?"

Nina looked at the gentle waves breaking on the white sand, the streetlights casting a golden glow on the serene beach. Catarina. Nina. "Actually, I don't know."

Jade stopped and faced Nina. "You don't know? You need to find out. My mother said names are special, just like people. How come you don't know the meaning of yours?" Her eyes widened in disbelief.

The real issue wasn't that Nina didn't know the meaning of her name. She was lost, unaware of her identity.

CHAPTER 11

"Nina, let's pick up seashells." The girl bounced on the sidewalk, her arms flailing in the air.

"It's getting too dark to see the shells. We should head back home," Nina said, casting a glance at the dwindling light in the sky.

"So, let's walk on the pier." Jade pointed to a wooden pier which extended into the darkening water.

The girl took Nina's hand and tugged her toward the pier. They climbed the wooden steps and strolled hand in hand, mingling with other people who were savoring the unseasonably pleasant breeze.

"Parker likes to fish here. Sometimes, I come with him." Jade hummed a tune about fish.

Nina nodded, her mind counting the steps to the end of the pier, eager to return to the inn. A profound fatigue weighed on her. Just twenty-four hours earlier, she had bid farewell to her father, embarking on a journey with no set destination. The first day in Grace Harbor, to her surprise, had been remarkably pleasant. Jade was a wonderful host, someone who wouldn't press her for explanations about her past. Any form of pressure at the moment would be a tremendous stress, and she needed, more than ever, to escape her past.

A chill went up Nina's arms. Darkness was creeping in. The pier and the boardwalk turned into a shadowy expanse. She tried focusing on Jade's chatter about fishing, but her anxiety escalated. The soft lapping of the waves against the posts seemed like murmurs from the past. The now dark sea threatened to swallow her.

"Nina, your hands are so clammy." Jade released the woman's hand and patted hers dry on her sweater.

"Just not a fan of the dark." Her mouth was dry, as if she'd eaten sand. "Let's go back, okay?"

Jade didn't oppose. She bounced on her feet toward the street, ignoring Nina's panic.

Back at the inn, Nina thanked Jade for the stroll. "We can do this more often if you'd like. When it's light out."

"Okay." Jade started toward the back door. She turned to Nina. "I'll find out the meaning of your name. It's important to know."

Nina thanked her. "I'm curious."

Jade waved goodbye and left. Nina climbed the stairs, legs feeling heavy and chest tight.

As she opened the door, a strange feeling struck her, as if someone had been waiting inside. She turned on the light and stepped in, peering under the bed and inside the closet. With mounting anxiety, she opened the drawer and checked the envelope with the money—still untouched. She inspected the bathroom and sighed with relief.

Rushing through her evening routine, Nina slid beneath the covers in her nightshirt and sent a brief message to her father.

Everything's fine.

***

The sensation of someone touching her face was overwhelming. Nina swatted at the air and turned to the other side of the bed. The touch continued. Between consciousness and oblivion, she struggled to open her eyes, which felt glued shut. She let out muffled cries as though someone was pressing a pillow against her face. She flailed her arms and tried to scream. Desperate, she thrust her body upward and forward, finally waking up. Her heart pounded, and her breath came in painful gasps.

With trembling hands, she turned on the bedside lamp and looked around. Nothing out of place. She threw the covers aside and got out of bed, her nightshirt drenched in sweat. Rushing to the bathroom, she flicked on the light and searched the small room. Nothing. Nina looked at herself in the mirror and ran her fingers through her tangled hair. She looked as though she had been in a street fight. She turned on the faucet and splashed cold water on her face. Bracing herself on the edge of the sink, she took deep breaths, making a colossal effort to calm her racing heart.

Worse than sleeping with the enemy was sleeping alone with the feeling the enemy was nearby.

Nina ambled to the window and slid it up. The cold, salty air hit her chest, chilling the damp nightshirt. Hands on the windowsill, she steadied herself despite the shivers. The street below was quiet. The dark yard with its gazebo was still. No strange sounds, just the usual nighttime noises and the whisper of the waves.

Tranquility-by-the-Sea. The inn was serene, but Nina's chest was agitated, and her mind filled with intrusive noises. For a moment, she was swept back to her opulent home. She roamed through the dark hallways and found herself in the bedroom. Nina tried to erase the memory, but it was stronger than her resolve.

After everything she had endured, had terror come to visit her in the form of panic attacks? Nina had read about it. They often hit after the immediate danger had passed, adrenaline flooding the system, numbing the senses. Panic surfaced as the body began to process what had happened. That must be it. Nina was in shock. Shock from all she had been through at Anderson's hands. All the shame, anger and humiliation were crashing down on her like ghosts tormenting Scrooge. Those were her ghosts.

Tears flowed as a natural consequence of this delayed reaction. Nina cried and cried. Her tears fell onto the yard below the window. Perhaps they would nourish the grass and the bushes. Perhaps they would kill whatever they touched like in Hawthorne's Rappaccini's Daughter.

Nina wiped her eyes with the long sleeve. Leaning against the window, she breathed slowly. A shadow in the yard startled her, causing her to leap back, slide down the window shut, and draw the curtains. Her heart raced again. It was a man, without a doubt.

Parting the curtain a little, she peeked out. The man crossed the yard and circled the inn, disappearing around the back of the house. Given the man's height, it couldn't be Anderson. The figure was tall, and her ex-husband, despite his delusions of superiority, was of average height.

Fear played tricks, Nina tried to convince herself. Just in case, she took the desk chair and wedged it against the door handle.

She returned to bed, hoping for a few more hours of sleep if her mind could stop bringing up painful memories. She needed a clear head for the following morning. Bank. Job. Those were her priorities.

The night noises seemed amplified, but Nina forced her thoughts in other directions. She was starting her life anew and had a chance to do it right. After years of captivity, witnessing the worst in someone, she believed she had gained some wisdom. The survival instinct had taught her caution and patience. Nina needed to win, to prove to herself that she could live with self-confidence, which Anderson had crushed like a bug under his shoe. Perhaps more coincidences would occur, and good things would come her way. She should feel hopeful, but her nerves were still frayed. She felt vulnerable.

I can do it. Tomorrow is a new day.

CHAPTER 12

T he buttery layers of the croissant melted in her mouth. Breakfast had become Nina's favorite meal. As the flaky chunks of the pastry dissolved in her mouth, she thought of the trip she and Anderson had taken to Rome. But the popular croissant and cappuccino breakfast in the *Città Eterna*, the Eternal City, hadn't been part of Nina's menu. The tantalizing morning aromas had been beyond reach for her.

Well, not anymore. Not in Grace Harbor.

She had been up at dawn, showered and ready to conquer Grace Harbor. Despite her panic attack in the middle of the night, Nina had slept well.

Looking around the empty dining-room, she took deep breaths in between bites. The aroma of coffee drifted into the room. It was too early for the other guests to rise, Esther had explained, after directing Nina to the dining-room.

She sipped the frothy cappuccino and planned her day. First, she would walk along Main Street to explore job opportunities in the shops and restaurants. Then, she'd go to the bank to deposit the money, which still troubled her conscience because of its source. She told herself Anderson owed her far more than money. The sum was a beginning toward making up for years of abuse and mistreatment.

"Glad you're enjoying your breakfast." Esther approached Nina's table. Her hair was pulled back, highlighting her well-defined face with almond-shaped eyes.

"This croissant is wonderful." She pointed to the crumbs on her plate.

"I'll ask Julie to get you another." Esther smiled and headed toward the kitchen.

Nina gratefully accepted the additional croissant the young server brought her. With her stomach full, she returned to the bedroom, brushed her teeth, grabbed her backpack, and headed out, deciding which direction to take. She started at the end of Main Street, where a small park welcomed early visitors, mainly elderly people with checkers boards.

At that hour, some restaurants were still closed. Nina visited two cafes, but they didn't need help. The same was true at a hardware store. It seemed pointless to inquire at the beauty salon or the pet shop. The ice cream parlor was closed, and there was no sign of 'Help Wanted.'

Beth's Bistro was bustling with activity, the air filled with the lively chatter of early risers.

Nina asked Simone if they were hiring. "I can do anything." At least she could cook well, something she learned under pressure.

With a tray under her arm, the young woman shook her head. "Sorry. Most tourists have already left for the season."

Nina sighed. It wasn't going to be as easy as she hoped. "That's alright. I'll keep looking." She headed for the door when Simone called her back.

"It's still early, but try Love at Second Sight," Simone suggested, pointing to the street. "A few doors down. They open in an hour. Why don't you take a walk on the beach while you wait? It's beautiful and peaceful at this time of the year."

"Good idea. Thanks." Nina hoped to boost her spirits by the prospect of landing a job at Love at Second Sight. She said goodbye to Simone and took the street leading to the beach.

The boardwalk was as expected: a few health-conscious people jogging, walking, biking, or strolling with their furry friends. The soft morning sun cast its light over the scene as the milky foam of the waves gently lapped at the white, soft sand, bringing seaweed and covering the shells. Ahead, Nina saw the pier, where some fishermen waited for their catch. In the daylight, everything looked peaceful.

Breathing in the sea air, she headed in that direction. The worn boardwalk had a thin layer of sand, blown in by the wind. Nina walked on, occasionally glancing at the fishing lines disappearing into the green water. She reached the end of the pier, where it opened into a wide square area. Some benches faced the railing. Nina sat down and watched the seagulls fight with the fishermen for their meal of the day. When one of the fishermen pulled in his line, three birds swooped down, trying to snatch what he hauled from the sea.

On the horizon, a few boats floated lazily. Nina felt the tension from the previous night dissipate. She stretched out her arms on the back of the bench and let the weak autumn sun warm her face. She unzipped the hoodie and looked up to the blue sky. Her curly hair swayed with the breeze, giving her a gentle head massage.

A tall man in shorts and a navy-blue windbreaker came into view. Nina straightened up on the bench and crossed her arms. The fisherman wore a hat with a few hooks pinned to the brim. He carried a cooler and his fishing gear. As he passed by Nina, he smiled and said good morning. She nodded. For a moment, she noticed something in his eyes that caught her attention, though she couldn't quite place it.

"Perfect morning for fishing," the man said, setting down the cooler and preparing his rod and hook. He smiled at Nina.

She prepared to leave if he came too close. He must have noticed her guarded expression because he shrugged and focused on his task. Soon, he cast his line into the water.

Checking the time on her phone, Nina sent a brief message to her father, saying she was job hunting, and headed back to Main Street. It wasn't wise to linger on the pier with so much money in her backpack.

On Main Street, Nina went straight to Love at Second Sight. The 'We Are Open' sign swung with the breeze, welcoming customers to step inside. She clasped her hands, cracking her knuckles. This might be one of her last chances for a job in Grace Harbor. The prospect of having to leave Grace Harbor gave her a sense of melancholy. The streets, the boardwalk, the inn and Beth's Bistro had become familiar to her.

Nina whispered a small prayer. Maybe God's helpline wasn't too busy that morning. She approached the glass door and let a woman with a baby in her arms exit first. The bell jingled as Nina pushed the door open.

"Coming," a female voice called from the back of the shop.

Before Nina could place the familiar voice, Grace appeared from the door behind the counter. "Look at what the seagulls brought in." The woman raised her arms as if to give Nina a hug, then quickly lowered them. "Nice to see you again. How can I help you?"

"You work here?" Perhaps another fortunate coincidence that might land her a job.

Grace laughed. "I'd say yes. It belongs to me and my dear husband, Abel."

Now that was quite a coincidence. Or an answer to her prayer. "Should I be surprised?" Nina smiled.

Grace laughed, came out from behind the counter and took Nina's hands. "Welcome to the Little Shop of Broken Hearts. I'm Grace Jenkins, proud owner of this shop."

"Little Shop of Broken Hearts? But the sign says—" Nina pointed to the door.

"Oh, yes. Love at Second Sight—that's the official name, but everyone in Grace Harbor knows it as the Little Shop of Broken Hearts." Grace led Nina to the corner with bookshelves and a cozy seating area. A dark-skinned man with salt-and-pepper hair was reading a hardcover book.

"A bit of a sad name, don't you think? But who doesn't have a broken heart in some way?" Grace swept her uneven bangs to the side.

Nina moved closer to one bookshelf and scanned the titles, most of which were classics. She sighed. Broken heart. Hers wasn't just broken. It was shattered and trampled. "Grace, I wonder if—"

The woman pointed to the man reading. "This is Abel, my husband. Honey, this is Nina."

Nina looked at him, and something in his gaze seemed off. Abel set the book on the coffee table and extended his slender arm to Nina.

"Nice to meet you, I'm Abel."

"Nice to meet you." She frowned when he repeated his name and shook his warm, big hand.

"What's your name?" he asked.

Grace tapped her husband's shoulder. "Nina as I just said."

Maybe the man had hearing issues. He seemed older or less energetic than his wife. Grace guided Nina to the counter, where she completed a transaction with a woman who had just bought a plant pot. Nina waited for the woman to leave before returning to the topic that brought her to the shop.

"I'm looking for a job, but no luck so far. I wonder if you could help me?"

For a moment, Nina thought Grace hadn't understood. The woman looked at her with a somewhat inscrutable expression, cocking her head, studying Nina's face.

"What brought you here?" Grace asked.

"I'm looking for a job." She frowned.

"What brought you to Grace Harbor?"

What was that supposed to mean? Grace had given her the train ticket. Did she forget their meeting at the station? Or did she want to know something Nina wasn't ready to reveal? "A coincidence brought me here. Remember the train station and the ticket?"

Grace furrowed her brow. "There's no such thing as coincidences."

Nina swallowed hard. She thought about leaving, but really needed a job or some help. She wasn't prepared for philosophical conversations about coincidences and fate. Grace was well known in the town and might know of available positions. So, Nina considered some answers before responding, "I came seeking a peaceful life." A straightforward but vague answer, non-committal.

Grace softened her expression. "I don't mean to embarrass you. I'm actually looking for help. From what I understand, you're just passing by. I need someone who will commit."

Commitment. Nina had just ended the most serious commitment a person could make—marriage. The commitment was broken despite her best intentions to maintain it. She had stayed in it for six long and painful years. That breakup was a blemish on her personal history. What would Grace think if she learned Nina had broken a sacred promise? Still, she needed a job. The less she had to handle Anderson's dirty money, the better. But how much commitment did Grace expect? How much was Nina willing to give?

And what if she ended up hating Grace Harbor and its residents? On the surface, the small town seemed pleasant, but what lay beneath? A commitment would force Nina to engage with the community. Hiding away in the inn would only suggest she had something to conceal. Grace cocked her head again, waiting for a response.

"How long is this commitment?" Nina asked.

"Long enough for you to get to know Grace Harbor and decide if you want to stay or leave."

Nina didn't quite understand what that meant or why Grace was asking it of her. However, since the commitment didn't have a set time frame, Nina considered she could accept the offer. If things didn't work out, she could tell Grace she had learned enough and decided to leave. That seemed reasonable, didn't it?

"I'll accept the commitment, then." A chill ran down Nina's spine. It felt as if she were signing a pact in her own blood, and if she broke it, something terrible might happen. Nina wasn't superstitious, but something about the proposal unsettled her. Maybe there was a catch, or worse, a trap.

CHAPTER 13

Nina opened an account at the bank but decided against depositing Anderson's money. It would raise suspicion. With a job, she wouldn't need to touch any more of that money. Grace had shown generosity by offering the newcomer a job and assisting with the banking issues.

A new chapter was beginning. Nina was excited about the job, and she would return the next day to talk with Grace and get more details about her tasks. She would do a little of this and that: handling the register, cleaning the shop, organizing stock, and more. Grace had referred to Nina's arrival as a miracle, saying she was considering delegating a few of the chores as she needed time to care for her husband. Grace hadn't discussed Abel's condition, and Nina didn't want to intrude.

On her way to Tranquility, Nina reflected on Grace's words about her arrival being a miracle. She disagreed. What had happened at the train station seemed more like a big coincidence. Nina had missed the train, Grace had shown up with a ticket, end of story. It was far from a miracle. Perhaps Grace liked to spiritualize things; Nina remembered that her father had the same habit.

She had long ago discarded the possibility of miracles happening, when her mother passed away. During the few hours she was in a coma, Nina had prayed with all her heart and might. When the doctor came with the news, Nina's heart had turned to stone. Her mom had been her best friend. She'd understood her daughter's low self-esteem and anxiety, as well as the struggles of teenage years marked by countless zits resembling pomegranate seeds. Tanya had dried Nina's tears when she didn't have anyone to take her to the prom. She had talked about self-worth and how God had made Nina special in so many ways. But feeling like the ugly duckling hadn't helped Nina's understanding of self-worth and value.

Maybe her faith hadn't been that great. God didn't listen, didn't see her. Hadn't the past six horrendous years been proof of that?

She now had a job despite the indefinite commitment attached to it.

Nina stopped by her room and sent a message to her father, sharing the good news. He wanted to know where she was, and Nina promised to give more details later on a video call.

Back at the reception area, which had remained empty since she arrived, Nina looked around and headed to the small room with bookshelves. A beam of sunlight streamed in, illuminating dust particles and highlighting the shell-shaped chair. She picked a book at random and sank into the cozy chair. Outside, the spruces formed a bluish wall, blocking the view of the street. Nina felt like she was in a special hideaway, like the secluded places she'd created for herself as a child, where she carried her books and toys. Tranquility-by-the-Sea was indeed a haven.

As she flipped through a poetry book, Nina read a verse here and there. An hour later, a familiar voice interrupted her quiet time.

"Nina." Jade pranced in, carrying a thick book with a leather cover. She plopped herself in another armchair. "I found your name." She placed the volume on the coffee table and flipped through its thick pages with her short fingers, the rustling sound of the paper traveling in the air. "Nina, He-brew name... Heb-rew... Hebrew," she glanced at Nina, smiled, and continued, "difficult word. Hebrew name meaning 'God was gracious and showed favor. Protector of feri-ferti-fertility and the sea.'" With a joyful face, Jade stood up and placed the book in Nina's lap. "I don't know what some of these words mean, but they sound neat."

Nina scanned the page. God being gracious seemed more like an irony. "How interesting. Now I'm near the sea and can protect it."

Jade knelt beside Nina and rested her arms on her lap. "I asked my mom what gracious means, and she said it's when God gives us what we don't deserve, like when Parker gave me the bike after I disobeyed him and called him mean."

In recent years, Nina had received little from God. Everything had come from Anderson, a kind of god in his own perception. She was starting all over, getting things herself, taking care of herself. "And where is your bike?"

Jade took off her sparkling headband, ran her fingers through her loose hair, and put the headband back on. "In the garage. Parker has a bike too, and you can use it. He doesn't mind."

"Maybe I should talk to Parker and ask."

"My mom said Parker is gracious; he gives us things even when we don't deserve them." Jade's smile brightened her round face.

So, Parker was almost a god himself! Nina was curious to meet such a virtuous figure. She held her tongue to keep from making a sarcastic remark. "How nice."

"Jade," Esther called from the reception area. "Are you bothering the guest?"

The girl ran to the door and stuck her head out. "No, Mom. I'm showing Nina the name book." Jade returned, grabbed the book, and sat down in the armchair, legs dangling.

Esther came in, holding an iPad. "If Jade is bothering you, just let me know." She winked.

"Not at all. We were talking about my name." Nina watched as mother and daughter exchanged smiles.

"And about Parker," Jade said.

"Hey, is someone gossiping about me?" A deep voice reverberated from the reception area, and soon a tall man with dark, straight hair entered.

Jade leaped from the armchair and threw herself at the man, hugging him around the waist. "Parker. When did you get here?"

Nina watched the scene and wondered when was the last time she had embraced someone with such enthusiasm and affection. Her father, when she was a child. Anderson, before he revealed his true colors.

The man lifted Jade and spun her around. "My precious pebble, I got back late last night and went fishing this morning."

The fisherman at the pier earlier. His eyes were identical to Esther's. Siblings? Nina watched the scene.

Esther interrupted the display of affection by tapping Parker on the shoulder. "This is Nina, our new guest, or should I say, new Grace Harbor resident."

Parker put Jade down and offered his hand to Nina, who took it hesitantly. "Nice to meet you. I hope you're enjoying your stay."

"I just arrived, but yes, everything is lovely." Nina felt uneasy. Despite Jade's positive comments about Parker, she would still need time to trust another man. A long time.

"So, are you going to make Grace Harbor your home sweet home?" The man smiled, showing his white, even teeth against his tanned face.

"I haven't decided yet." Brief answer. If Nina hadn't talked so much to Anderson at the vending machine the day her dad was undergoing surgery, if she had smiled politely and returned to the O.R. waiting room, she wouldn't be in this situation.

Esther sat in the chair opposite Nina's. "Have you found a job?"

Heat rose from Nina's neck to her face. "Actually, I did, at Grace's little shop."

"The Little Shop of Broken Hearts," Parker said.

Jade took Nina's hand. "Don't worry, the hearts don't really break. It's just that many people who go there are sad. That's what Auntie Grace told me."

Nina held back a laugh. She was the perfect hire to manage the Little Shop of Broken Hearts.

Esther ran her fingers through her daughter's hair. "People aren't sad, they just have problems."

"I start tomorrow."

"So, can we go bike riding later?" Jade asked Nina, turning to her mother and Parker.

"Why not?" Esther said.

Approaching Parker, Jade took his hands and shook them. "Can Nina use your bike? I told her you're gracious."

He let out a hearty laugh that filled the small room. "What a way to charm your uncle."

"What's charm?" she asked.

Parker pinched the girl's nose. "To convince someone by saying nice things."

Esther stood up and started toward the door. She turned back to Nina. "These two are a great love story."

"And how could I not love my precious pebble?" He tickled the girl, who ran away and jumped into the armchair, laughing.

"You're a silly uncle," she said.

"And you are a shiny pebble," he replied.

Nina watched as more playful teasing unfolded. Esther left, shaking her head and muttering something.

"Jade, what time are we bike-riding?" Nina stood up and placed the poetry book back on the shelf.

"Four o'clock." The girl picked up the heavy name book.

"I'll leave the bikes in front of the cottage. Hope you enjoy the ride." Parker waved to Nina and left the room, followed by Jade, who was calling her uncle more unusual names.

In her bedroom, Nina grabbed a notepad with the inn's letterhead and wrote the meaning of her name. She repeated the definition out loud, laughed, tossed the notepad into the drawer, and shut it. If a name reflected her present condition, what would that be?

Grace meant receiving without deserving. Giving to those who didn't deserve it, expecting nothing in return, without mistreating. Anderson demanded everything from Nina. What she received was based on merit, and in recent years, her merit score was negative, according to her husband.

Nina was a nomad in the desert of life, where no virtue grew, although that wasn't quite true. Patience and self-control had kept her from committing an act of violence. How many times had she considered washing Anderson's white shirts with the colored clothes? How many times had she plotted to replace his shampoo with her hair removal cream? And to use garlic paste instead of the detestable horseradish? So many times, she couldn't count. Maybe she had some virtues after all.

That was all in the past. A recent past, only two days ago, but still the past. The present and the future depended on her, and Nina was determined to give it her best so that Grace wouldn't regret hiring her. She would do everything in her power to deserve the new job and the pay.

The Little Shop of Broken Hearts. Nina hoped the nickname didn't bring more sorrow into her life, because her own heart needed repair.

CHAPTER 14

"Do you think this man is a detective?" Nina looked at her father's worried expression on the cellphone screen. Her anxiety grew.

"It's possible. My police instincts kicked in when I noticed him." Martin pressed the bridge of his nose.

Nina had returned from the bike ride with Jade and called her father to share the good news about her job. She and Jade had run into Grace on the way back to the inn, and the older woman had invited Nina to dinner at her house.

The joy of talking to her father faded as he told her he was being followed.

"Then I'd better not say where I am."

Martin shook his head. "I need to know so I can protect you. Anderson wouldn't harm me. He has too much to lose."

"A model citizen he is." She sneered.

"He built his reputation on that. He wouldn't get his hands dirty."

Anderson's hostility had left scars, imperceptible to others but deep in his wife's soul. He was a coward. "Maybe you're right. I'm in a town called Grace Harbor, New Hampshire. How I ended up here is a strange story, and I'll tell you later. I like it here already." Nina told her father about Esther and Jade. He laughed when Nina told him about the girl's book of names.

"I like her already. She makes you happy." He smiled.

"I like her innocence. I spent so many years surrounded by falsehood. It made me sad and cynical. Jade is genuine. I think I can learn from her how to be simpler." Nina spoke more about her new friend and described the quiet town.

Before hanging up, her father reassured her he would take care of himself and ask a police friend to find out more about the man following him.

When Nina got in the shower, the feeling of being watched returned. She knew it was foolish, but the anxiety was real.

***

The yellow house with white shutters had a little porch with two rocking chairs and pots of colorful flowers. It was a typical grandmother's house, where time seemed to have stopped, encapsulating the best of a pure world.

Nina climbed the wooden steps to the porch and rang the doorbell. She heard quick footsteps, and soon Grace appeared at the door. The aroma of bread danced in the cool night air, and Nina extended her hand, offering Grace a pot of hydrangea.

"Welcome, Nina." Grace took the gift. "Hydrangea. My companions in the kitchen."

"Thank you for having me."

"It's a pleasure, dear. Come in, come in. Abel is getting out of the shower and will be here soon."

Nina glanced around and felt at home. The living room was small, with antique furniture and crocheted items decorating the sofa, the two armchairs, and the coffee table. Colorful blankets were folded in a basket, and a braided rug covered the center of the room. Nina sat in the armchair and interlaced her fingers in her lap. She looked at the woman with her short, uneven bangs and smiled.

"Excited for your first day at work tomorrow?" Grace asked, still standing in the middle of the room with the flowerpot in her hands. Her yellow apron matched the yellow and white polka-dot dress.

"Excited and anxious."

"Anxious? How come?"

"Everything is new to me. I just got here, and I'm not sure where I fit in Grace Harbor. I get the impression that everyone knows each other, and I'm an intruder." Nina played with the hem of her gray sweater.

Grace sat on the arm of the sofa. "There are no intruders in Grace Harbor. Those who come here have an important reason."

Nina had arrived there by chance, and Grace knew that well. "I came by accident, didn't I?"

"You still think it's a coincidence?" The woman waved her hand dismissively. "No one stays in a place without a purpose."

And what could have been the purpose of living with an enemy? Nina didn't share Grace's philosophy, that much was certain. "I hope I can find out what my purpose is."

Slow footsteps from the hallway caught Nina's attention. Abel came into the living room.

Grace put the pot down on the coffee table, stood up and helped her husband to the other armchair. "Abel, this is Nina, remember? She's here to have supper with us."

Nina noted the man's empty eyes. "Good evening. Thank you for inviting me."

"Are you going to eat with us?" Abel frowned.

"Yes, she is." Grace squeezed her husband's shoulder. "You two chat while I check on the food." She left with the flowerpot.

Nina offered a faint smile to the elderly man, who was looking in her direction, but seemed not to see her. "Did you have a good day today?" The question sounded rehearsed. What would she say to a distracted or ill person? The man didn't respond. Nina shifted in the armchair and peered into the hallway, wishing Grace would return soon. The sound of pots indicated that the woman was busy. Nina made another attempt to spark a conversation. "What were you reading in the shop earlier?"

The man's eyes sparkled to life as if he had just noticed Nina for the first time. "Do you know Rip Van Winkle?"

Nina mentally pulled the files of high-school English classes. "By Washington Irving. Winkle sleeps and wakes up years later with a long beard."

"'The people were all so different, they seemed as if they had been asleep and had just awaked from a long dream.' I like this quote from Rip Van Winkle. Sometimes, my mind falls asleep. That's why I enjoy reading. It's always awake."

Nina's eyes burned. Abel, with his curly hair sprinkled with gray, gentle wrinkles around his eyes, spoke with confidence and calmness. Nina wished to hear more of his velvety voice. "What else do you like reading?"

"Anything that helps me grow and protects my mind. Reading feeds and protects the mind like fertilizers for plants. This kind of reading never corrupts the mind and the soul."

How long had it been since Nina had picked up a book and read it cover to cover? Anderson thought reading anything that wasn't medicine, politics, and finance was a waste of time. One day, he caught his wife reading a historical romance, which she kept in a shoebox. Anderson tore its pages, saying that it was the reading of an idle woman. He pulled Nina into his study, with its bookcase full of well-bound volumes, and yelled at her, saying true knowledge was on those shelves. After that, Nina gave up on fictional stories. Her own life was a dystopia, an absurd fantasy.

"I'd like to know more about this kind of reading. I saw there are classics in the shop." Nina leaned forward. She smiled when Abel nodded.

"I can tell you more about them." His rich and warm voice, like Morgan Freeman's, soothed Nina.

Grace returned to the room, announcing supper was served. She helped her husband up and invited Nina to join them. The dining room was just what Nina expected—an oval table with a floral tablecloth, chairs with vintage floral print, and a china cabinet filled with figurines.

They sat down, and Grace said a brief prayer. Nina bowed her head, recalling how her parents always prayed before a meal when she was growing up.

Living with Anderson had reinforced her skepticism, not only because his belief was in medicine and himself, but also because Nina had grown tired of calling out to God for help.

It was true that no one had forced her to marry Anderson, and her father had warned her against it. But what defenses did a person with clouded self-esteem have? Nina had never been popular in school, athletic, creative or funny, like her classmates and friends. In her teenage world, a person's importance was measured by popularity. Nina's life seemed simple, but her inner world was a mess. That was what Anderson needed to seduce the woman who he would mold in his image. A kind of Frankenstein. The problem was that the experiment went wrong, and Nina was an enormous disappointment to Anderson. The struggle against the scale, the lack of motivation to go to parties, and little social sophistication contributed to her downfall.

"Nina," Grace handed a dish of vegetables to her guest, "how are you managing at the inn?"

"It's all good. The room is comfortable. Jade has kept me busy; we've gone out twice already." She scooped a small serving of green beans and baby carrots glistening with butter, paused for a moment, then scooped some more.

"Jade has endless energy." Grace laughed. "Boredom bolts like a roadrunner the moment she shows up."

Nina laughed and dished a piece of the juicy chicken thigh with rosemary. "She's a bit like you. If you're like the mayor, she's a councilor."

Grace smile. "In Grace Harbor, we all know each other in one way or another. Our paths cross."

How many paths would Nina cross? She couldn't draw attention to herself. Her story was hers, and few would understand her reasons for fleeing. "That seems to be the case."

After supper, Nina helped Grace tidy up the kitchen. With a cup of coffee in hand, the guest followed the host to the living room, where Abel was reading a hardcover book. The work at Love at Second Sight was the topic of conversation between Grace and her new employee. The shop had been in operation for over twenty years, first selling gently used clothes and later expanding to other products and services. Nina was caught up in Grace's excitement as she talked about her business. When Abel left the room, saying he was tired, Grace confided in Nina Abel had dementia. She explained the books were his reconnection with the world around him.

"He needs help with simple tasks, like brushing his teeth. Not that he can't use a toothbrush, but because he goes into the bathroom and forgets why he is there," Grace said. "He never remembers to take his medication. He gets antsy when I remind him of things or when he thinks he lost something, like his favorite book or watch. It's good for him to be in the shop and meet the reading group. He can quote long texts, and feels relaxed because of it."

Nina studied Grace's tired face and weak smile. What would it be like to care for someone who gradually lost touch with reality? In what horrible bubble had Nina lived the past few years that she hadn't noticed the difficulties of others? There were Grace and Abel. At the inn, Esther and Jade. Nelson and Celia, who had lost a child. Nina had learned from Anderson that people dug their own graves with wrong decisions. Grace, Esther, and Celia hadn't produced the difficulties they faced. Anderson was judgmental and wanted to fix everyone, not just with a scalpel. He had answers for everyone's problems. If someone confided in him about their worries, he would suggest a quick fix, without the slightest empathy. Arrogance and pride were his counselors.

Listening to Grace, Nina wanted to flee from yet another thing: her foolishness and her misguided thoughts about others. And about herself. Perhaps, even in difficult situations, people could smile. Grace smiled. Esther smiled. Jade was pure joy with her fun shoelaces and good humor.

Were the events of the past two days more than mere coincidences after all? Would she find the motivation to smile again in Grace Harbor? There were practical matters to address first, like detaching herself from Anderson. The word divorce sounded ugly to her ears. Yet how could she remain tied to her husband, the man who treated her like a second-class human being? Nina thought of Grace's shop name: Love at Second Sight. Would someone look at Nina with empathy, giving her the chance to reclaim her identity?

Without a formal separation from Anderson, Nina risked having her new life interrupted by his absurd demands. He wouldn't rest until he had avenged the humiliation Nina had caused him. She knew Anderson. The most important thing to him, in all circumstances, was to keep his pride. The Bible said that pride went before destruction, but what Nina saw was a man without scruples, prospering.

After thanking Grace for the pleasant evening, Nina took a walk on the beachfront boardwalk, trying to relieve the pressure building in her chest. When anxiety surged like a shadow, she returned to the inn. She needed some time alone with herself.

She pulled out the notepad from the dresser drawer and jotted down more thoughts. Perhaps it would help if she bought a journal and wrote regularly. Abel organized his jumbled thought in reading. Nina could do the same with writing.

She scribbled some random notes but came to no conclusion about her problems. She put the pad away and got ready for bed. A terrible sensation of being watched resurfaced. She could feel Anderson getting closer and closer.

CHAPTER 15

Curled up in the shell-shaped chair in the inn, Nina turned another page of a short story book. Seated on the cream carpet, Jade rested her arms on the coffee table and did her homework. This was Nina's favorite routine after work. Three weeks had passed since her arrival in Grace Harbor. Her weekday ritual included a quick breakfast of croissant and cappuccino at the inn, various tasks at work, a light supper at Beth's Bistro, a relaxing shower and time in the reading nook. When Jade didn't have homework, the two would go out for a stroll or ride their bikes.

Esther thanked Nina for her connection with Jade. She said the girl waited for Nina with bubbling excitement so they could hang out together. In truth, it was Nina who was grateful for Jade's company. Besides being funny, she had a perspective on life that was profound, though simple. Perhaps the girl didn't even realize that her words had a significant impact on Nina's life. No demands, no judgments, just genuine friendship.

Jade erased a column of words from the spelling worksheet, brushing the eraser shavings aside. She brought the pencil to her lips and glanced at Nina. "My handwriting is messy." A pout appeared on her face.

Nina lowered the book onto her lap and leaned forward. "Can I see?" She took the worksheet and studied the letters. "I don't see anything wrong. Why did you erase that whole column?"

Jade shrugged. "I'll just do it again." She took the paper back, but her gaze remained on Nina. "Why do you only wear sad clothes?"

Nina looked down at her jeans, gray T-shirt, and black hoodie. None of the expensive shiny fabrics from her former wardrobe. Nina had always wondered what Anderson saw in her when they met. He loved the company of beautiful women. Perfect women on the outside. She had asked him once. He had assessed her with contempt. "You're a blank slate. I can perform any miracle with these hands," he'd said, admiring his hands. Anderson transformed Nina into Catarina using needles, lasers, chemicals, and other methods like those used by Aylmer in Hawthorne's The Birthmark.

Trying to erase the memories, Nina sighed. "I prefer plain clothes."

Jade dropped the pencil on the table. "But it's all black, white, and gray. Don't you like colors?"

Once, her clothes had had color, but her life had been monochromatic. Nina shrugged. "Not for my clothes."

"Why don't you buy some things at Aunt Grace's shop?"

Nina didn't mind Jade's questions. She was curious and explored the world in her own way. In fact, Nina had imagined herself wearing the vintage clothes from Love at Second Sight's collection with its timeless elegance and classic charm. She had liked a pastel blue and white plaid dress with a flared skirt and high waist that had just arrived at the shop. Nina had held it up to her body and looked in the mirror. It seemed fitting for Grace Harbor's unique charm. "I think what I have is fine for now. I don't go out much."

Jade pointed to Nina's black sneakers. "Do you want one of my shoelaces?" Without waiting for a response, the girl dashed out of the room and returned minutes later with a pair of light blue shoelaces. "Here. I think blue looks good on you."

"Jade," the unmistakable voice of Esther called from the reception area. "Don't disturb Nina."

Nina and Jade laughed. Esther kept a keen ear out for her daughter when she was around. It had become customary for her to ask if the girl was bothering Nina, and for Nina to reply that she wasn't. It had become their own special kind of banter. Nina felt like family. Well, at least wanted to think so.

On two occasions, Esther invited her guest to supper at the cottage. Jade insisted Nina should eat with them every evening, but Nina quickly declined. She didn't want to intrude on the family's routine. Besides, she had learned Parker also lived in the cottage, but spent some days away managing the family's other inn, Tranquility-by-the-Lake. So, they never bumped into each other when Nina had supper at the cottage.

"Mom, Nina and I are talking about clothes," the girl replied.

"You need to finish your homework." Esther's tone was firm.

Jade shook her head, making her typical pout, and went back to her worksheet. Nina opened the book and continued reading a story. Four pages later, she lowered the book again and looked at Jade, who was erasing the words she had just written.

"How about going for a walk on the boardwalk? You can relax and finish this later. You don't have much left. I'll talk to your mom." Nina decided Anderson's ghosts wouldn't stop her from being free in Grace Harbor.

The girl dropped her pencil and stood up. "I'll go get my jacket. Be right back." She ran out, telling her mother she was going out with Nina.

Esther thanked Nina for taking care of Jade. "Some days are harder for her. Harder for me too when I don't have much time to help her." She rested her elbows on the counter. "It's a bit harder when Parker is away."

Nina's eyes burned. Exhaustion etched into Esther's face. How many sleepless nights had she gone through, worrying about her daughter? How raw was the ache of Jade's father's absence?

She grasped Ether's hands and squeezed them, compassion warming up her heart. "I'm here." Nina's chin quivered. She felt compelled to help Esther in her effort to care for a special needs child. Yes, the world was a bigger place than the one Anderson had confined Nina in with his oppression. There was life outside. Not a perfect life. Just life that happened in so many ways.

"Thank you." Esther squeezed Nina's hand back, her eyes moist.

Jade broke the brief, but heartfelt conversation. She bounced into the reception area, announcing she was ready to go out.

Hand in hand, Nina and Jade left the inn and walked down the street to the boardwalk. The silvery light of the full moon bathed the beach. The early fall chill hung in the air, crisp and invigorating. A family came out of the candy shop, eating cotton candy. Jade asked for one. Nina ordered a blue and a pink, at Jade's suggestion. They walked on the pier, savoring the sugary clouds.

The unsettling sensation of being followed resurfaced, and Nina's adrenaline surged. Grace Harbor was a serene town. She trusted the residents. But something was off. Maybe it was just her, the fear of returning to her old life.

Nina scanned the surroundings. Only a few residents were walking their dogs, biking or sitting on the benches along the boardwalk and the pier.

Oblivious to Nina's gnawing concern, Jade tugged at her pink cotton candy, her small fingers pulling it closer to her mouth. She paused her humming as she enjoyed the sweet treat.

Nina's legs froze at the sight of a shadow looming at the end of the pier. Before she could even suggest to Jade they head back, the girl had already dashed ahead.

"Jade, Jade, come back!" The ocean's vastness swallowed her voice.

Nina ran, waving her cotton candy in the air. The shadow shifted to face them. Nina's throat tightened, struggling to breathe. "Jade."

Jade sprinted toward the shadow, which lifted her into the air. Nina's heart raced as she recognized the familiar figure. Parker. Relief flooded through her. She halted and leaned against the railing, feeling a wave of dizziness. "I'm paranoid," she murmured to herself.

"Nina, Parker is here." Jade pulled her uncle by the hand and brought him to Nina, who was trying to steady herself on her shaky legs.

"Are you okay?" he asked.

"Afraid Jade would fall." She gasped.

Parker bent down to Jade's eye level. "My precious pebble, don't do this again. I know you saw me, but what if you had mistaken me for a stranger? What did I say about not approaching strangers?"

"I should never go with someone I don't know. But I knew it was you," she protested.

Nina tossed her cotton candy in the nearby trash can. "Alright, Jade. We'll be more careful next time." She straightened up from the railing. The world swirled around her. The adrenaline rush kept her trembling. She drew in the salty sea air, hoping it would anchor her to the present moment.

"Nina, what happened?" Parker came closer. He bent his arm and offered it to her. "Hold on here. Let's go back."

"Sorry, Nina." Jade sniffed and clung to her uncle's other arm.

"It's alright." It wasn't true. Her legs felt like jelly. She hesitated before reaching for Parker's arm, but she wouldn't be able to get to the inn without support. The feeling of being watched lingered.

They walked back, arms linked, leaving the pier and the frightening experience behind. Parker slowed his pace when Nina lowered her head. Everything was spinning. It might have been the excess sugar combined with adrenaline. At the inn's door, Jade went in first. Esther looked alarmed when Parker entered with Nina.

"What happened? Nina's pale." Esther stepped out from behind the counter.

"I made Nina sick." Jade sniffed.

Parker guided Nina to the reading nook and helped her settle into her favorite chair. Gradually, her vision adjusted to the warm light of the room.

She looked at Jade, who was almost in tears. "It's not your fault. I got scared."

Esther asked her daughter to bring water for Nina. She perched on the edge of an armchair while Parker remained on his feet.

"I don't know where you lived before, but don't worry; Grace Harbor is safe," Esther said.

Nina drank half of the glass of water Jade brought. "I really need to get used to it." No need to explain where she came from. And it wasn't the big city that caused her fear.

"Feeling better?" Parker asked.

The family's concern touched Nina. Maybe because she was already feeling emotionally fragile, tears rolled down her face. Jade sat beside her and hugged her. The two nestled into the round chair, seeking mutual comfort.

"I promise I won't run off again, Nina."

Nina gently stroked Jade's head and placed a tender kiss on it. Esther and Parker watched, their expression tender. As Jade buried her face in Nina's chest, the room fell into a deep, serene silence. Nina closed her eyes. The world around her came to a standstill. The gentle warmth of Jade's body eased Nina's shakiness, wrapping her in a soothing calm.

Some time later, Esther stood up. "Well, it's getting late. Bedtime for Jade."

Taking the cue, Parker approached his niece and pulled her by the arm. "My precious pebble, story time. Which one do you want?"

"The one about the unicorn." She grabbed her uncle's hand.

"The unicorn it is." Parker looked at Nina with concern. "I hope you have a good night."

"Thank you. I'm feeling better." She was surprised at how the tender moment had erased her fear.

Parker left with Jade, and Esther helped Nina stand up. She apologized once more for her daughter's behavior. Nina assured her it wasn't Jade's fault.

"Sometimes the past has a way of catching up with us." Nina looked into Esther's companionate eyes. She wasn't ready to share her life with anyone. Not just yet.

CHAPTER 16

As the weeks passed, Nina marked her second month in Grace Harbor by treating herself to a dress in a brighter color from the vintage collection. Jade would approve.

After closing the shop, with Grace busy at the register, Nina slipped into the fitting room with the dress. She admired her reflection, pleased with how the lilac shade with tiny white dots complemented her. It was comfortable and matched her cream Mary Jane shoes. She brought a hand to her lips, suppressing a laugh. The wife of the powerful Dr. Anderson Phillips wearing second-hand clothes.

Throwing the outfit she'd worn into a paper bag, Nina stepped out of the fitting room. Grace looked up from a pile of receipts and whistled. "It looks great on you. I like it."

"It'll be tough getting used to this style," she said, a hint of excitement in her voice. "But honestly, I've always dreamed of dressing like this—like in those fifties movies." She placed the bag on the floor and pulled her backpack from the hook on the wall.

Grace stepped out from behind the counter. "No more of that backpack. Come here." She walked over to the purse display near the shoe rack and picked out a classic one for Nina. "It's a gift."

Nina took the purse. It was her favorite from the new fall collection—smooth leather with clean lines and a discreet buckle. Perhaps Grace had noticed how she'd been eyeing the purse all day. Nina might even have redirected a customer to another purse earlier. "I'll pay for it."

"It's a gift, and I insist." Grace squeezed Nina's shoulder and winked.

Abel, who was reading a book in the shop's corner, glanced at the two women and returned his attention to the pages.

"Thank you." She ran her hand over the purse, feeling its softness.

"Are you having supper at Beth's bistro?" Grace gathered the receipts in her plump hands.

"I am. That's when I write in my new journal. I've always thought it intriguing when people write in cafes." Nina laughed and threw the backpack into the paper bag. She had bought the journal two weeks earlier, and writing had proven therapeutic. Simone always reserved a corner table at the bistro for Nina. She loved lingering there, savoring the feeling of being like a movie character, lost in thought, with a coffee mug by her side.

Nina waved Grace goodbye and stepped out onto the street, feeling the hem of the skirt brush against her leg. She smiled as she walked, catching a glimpse of herself in a shop window—curly hair framing a face she almost didn't recognize, wearing a beautiful dress. A rush of realization startled her. She was looking at herself, emerging from her ugly cocoon.

At the bistro, Simone, Celia, and Nelson complimented her outfit. After a quick chat with them, Nina headed to her table at the back of the restaurant. Simone brought her the dish of the day: roasted chicken and potatoes, Nina's favorite. She ate the meal with pleasure. Half an hour later, with a slice of apple pie and a steaming cup of coffee in front of her, Nina reached into the backpack and pulled out her floral journal. She opened it and reread the entry about her name. Ever since Jade had explained its meaning, Nina couldn't shake the thought of receiving something undeserved. Grace—a gift without strings attached. Meeting Jade and Grace had been a true blessing. There were others too, like Esther, Abel, Simone, and Parker.

Nina wrote down the thought.

She ate the last morsel of pie, and Simone cleared the table. Nina focused on her journal. In the middle of another paragraph, a familiar voice interrupted her concentration. It was Parker.

"Found a nice little corner?" He smiled, his eyes narrowing more.

Nina looked up. He was so tall that even while standing, she had to tilt her head upward to meet his gaze. "I feel important writing in a bistro."

"You've Got Mail with Meg Ryan and Tom Hanks?"

"I think Meg Ryan read in a cafe, but something like that." Nina's memory reignited the frustration she felt toward Anderson's joyless grip on her life. To him, movies were a waste of time—at least for her. She toyed with the page of her journal, eager to continue spilling her reflections onto the paper. Meanwhile, the man in front of her stood as solid as the trees lining Main Street.

"Can I?" He pointed at the chair opposite from hers. Simone is finishing up packaging pastries for the inn.

"Sure." Nina massaged her tense neck from looking up.

Parker sat down. He straightened his black leather jacket, brushed his hair back, but it fell back onto his forehead. "Enjoying the work at the shop?"

"Very much. Grace has been spending more time with Abel, so I've been quite busy. Time flies by." She closed the journal and tapped the pen on the cover. "Esther said you have another inn, Tranquility-by-the-Lake."

"Yes. That was the first inn, built by our grandparents. They came to Grace Harbor from Korea and fell in love with the place. They opened the second one years later. That was 50 years ago. My parents managed the inns for a while but retired in Florida. Esther and I took over the business nine years ago."

"It must be an interesting job."

"It's nice to meet new people from all over. Where do you come from?"

Nina grabbed the purse and bag from the chair beside her and tossed the journal inside. Dangerous subject. To her relief, Simone arrived with Parker's order.

"Need a bag?" The young woman handed him three boxes of pastry.

Parker took the boxes and placed them on the table. "No, that's fine. Thanks."

"Can I get the check, Simone?" Nina asked.

"It's already been paid," the server said with a smile.

Nina looked at Simone with wide eyes and then at Parker, who shrugged. "Who paid?"

"I don't know. Beth said it's been taken care of." Simone shrugged, too.

Fear crept up Nina's legs to her waist, then crawled up her back and arms like icy claws sliding beneath her skin. Her heart raced. She jumped up, almost tipping her chair. "I need to go."

Parker grabbed the boxes. "Let's walk together."

The last thing Nina wanted was to walk alone. Who had settled her bill? She considered asking Beth, but an overwhelming need to lock herself in her room overcame her. Even if it meant enduring the nightmares. She wanted to sleep, wake up the next day and let the sun chase away the feeling of dread. Everything seemed to improve in the light of day.

Nina thanked Simone and headed for the door, zigzagging between the tables with few customers. Her feet felt heavy, as if the ground had some powerful glue preventing her from running away. Suddenly, her new dress didn't matter anymore. The new purse, the new shoes, nothing made sense. She needed her black hoodie, her regular jeans. The simple, dark clothes gave her security, a kind of camouflage in the dark night.

"Nina, wait." Parker came up beside her. "What happened?"

"I need to call my dad. He's waiting." It was worth a lie to run and hide.

The clear, starry night did little to lift Nina's spirits. Her feet quickened despite the weight of her legs, the leather soles of her new shoes hitting the pavement at a rapid pace. Nina felt Parker's gaze on her, as well as the daunting sensation of another pair of eyes watching from the shadows.

At the inn, Esther was talking to a couple. Nina hesitated for a moment, gripping the doorknob, her eyes scanning the room for anyone suspicious. When she let go, Parker gently pressed the door closed behind her. He set the pastries on the counter and motioned for her to follow him to the reading nook. She clutched her purse, but soon followed him. Parker turned on the light and closed the door. With the strap of her purse slipping off her shoulder, she hugged herself, trying to steady her trembling body.

"Nina, what's going on?" His tone was soothing.

"I think I'm just tired." She sat down in the armchair.

Parker pulled another chair closer to Nina. "Is someone causing trouble? Following you?"

"Why do you say that?" Her eyes widened.

"Your reaction in the bistro was like that night on the pier. Please, tell me if someone is bugging you. I want to help."

What would she say? That she felt her husband's presence? How would she explain that without giving away too much? "I don't know. Maybe it's just stress. I miss my dad."

"Could he come visit you?" He clasped his hands and leaned his body forward, concern etched into his face.

She needed her father more than ever, but the detective might follow him, and Anderson soon after. "Not right now."

"I understand." Parker rubbed his hands on his knees. "Nina, listen. I want to help. If you're uneasy walking home when it's dark, I can walk with you back to the inn. It's no trouble, and I'm usually around anyway."

A knot tightened in her throat. Her friends in Grace Harbor were generous in many ways, but she didn't want to exploit that. She was the mysterious outsider. "Appreciate it, but I need to manage on my own. I have to let go of this silly fear. I'm a grown woman, right?" She tried to sound upbeat.

Parker looked at her and nodded. "Then let's make a deal."

Nina tensed in the armchair. She had already committed to Grace, working at the shop for an indefinite period. What would Parker ask of her? "What deal?"

"Nothing much. Why don't you join us for supper at the cottage?"

She cocked her head. "Parker, you saw me at the bistro. I just ate."

He grinned with a playful squint. "I sure did, but the invitation is to join us every evening for supper. Jade will be thrilled. This was her suggestion, but Esther was concerned you might feel we are imposing."

A wave of relief washed over Nina, like a bucket of warm water rinsing away her fear. Dining alone and playing the damsel in distress had lost its appeal. Parker's invitation felt like a balm on her wounded soul. Nina loved Jade's fun companionship and Esther's supportive disposition. "I don't know. I think I'll be imposing."

"Anyone who stays in Grace Harbor for more than a month is family. Didn't you know?" He put on a fake expression of surprise.

"I guess I didn't get the memo on family ties in Grace Harbor." She smiled, amazed at how easily it came out.

"Well, now you know." He clapped his hands.

Esther walked into the room, hands pressed against her face. "Nina, what happened? You were pale when you arrived."

"Everything's fine," Parker said. "I just told Nina she's part of the large Grace Harbor family, and she's joining us at supper."

Nina felt grateful for his change of topic. Rehashing the event at the bistro would only bring back the tension. Despite the lingering uneasiness about the unknown person who paid her bill, her fear had subsided.

Esther smiled. "Jade will be thrilled to know she has an aunt."

Nina stood. "Thank you for everything."

"I'll walk you to your room," Parker said.

Nina nodded. Her legs still trembled, but Parker's presence beside her gave her confidence. It wasn't just the reassurance of safety that mattered, but also the comforting realization she could rely on her new family.

On the second floor, Nina retrieved the key from the purse. Parker took it from her and unlocked the door. He craned his neck, glancing around the room. To Nina, it was a silent reassurance that everything was under control.

He returned the key to her. "If you need anything, let me or Esther know. And if you want company coming back from work, just call me. You have my number." They had exchanged phone numbers on the way up from the reception area.

"I promise." She took the key and thanked Parker, her voice sounding firmer.

He stood still, studying Nina's face. She leaned against the doorjamb, hand on the knob. She recognized Parker's protective nature, the same care he showed toward Jade and Esther. It made her feel safe, like when she was younger, and her parents watched over her.

Parker raised his hand in a subtle wave, turned, and walked down the hallway.

CHAPTER 17

Nina straightened the dresses and shirts on their hangers, the metal clinking as she slid them along the rack. She then surveyed the shop and moved to the corner where the decorative items were displayed. With a duster, she cleaned the coffee tables, chairs, lamps, knick-knacks and other accents. Her gaze fell upon a set of glass figurines of sea creatures. She tucked the duster under her arm, her hand lingering over the little seahorse, dolphin and starfish. She fought the bitter memory of the crystal set Anderson told her to return, dismissing them as useless.

The glass set in front of her wasn't as fine as the one she'd loved, but it called to her. The little ornaments were hers to choose. No one would take them away this time.

Nina picked up the little glass creatures, cradling them in her hands as if rescuing real animals washed ashore. With tender care, she set them on the counter, claiming them as her own. She would add more pieces to her collection as they became available.

With a deep sense of satisfaction, she returned to work. As she dusted the rest of the furniture, Nina watched the group seated in the reading area. Grace had said Abel woke up in a good mood, eager to read poems to the customers.

Celia and Nelson listened as Abel recited several poems by Robert Frost. Nina remembered some poems from English classes, especially The Road Not Taken. Swinging the duster back and forth, in the same cadence as Abel's soft voice, she heard the first verses about a fork in the road on a wooded path, about how the poet had to choose between two diverging paths, and how that choice would shape his life.

Abel recited the poem to the small audience, his eyes distant and unfocused, moving beyond the pages before him. His voice carried the weight of the words as if they were threads of memory in the fading awareness of the world around him.

It was beautiful. Abel's voice, soft and silken, drifted through the shop, drawing Nina in. She knew the stanzas almost by heart, yet anticipated the ending's revelation. It was hard to believe she was the personification of the truth penned by Frost. Abel's intonation captured the essence of the lesson in the next verse, "Yet knowing how way leads on to way, I doubted if I should ever come back."

Nina rubbed her nose with the back of her hand. How well the poem represented what she had gone through at the train station. She insisted on everything being a coincidence, but in reality, she had accepted Grace's offer. Nina could have thanked her, purchased another ticket for the train she had missed, and taken the more traveled path. But here she was, in Grace Harbor, at the Little Shop of Broken Hearts, with broken people seeking restoration. Lately, Nina had been thinking about the possibility of something beyond coincidence guiding her towards a less common path. She was eager to take her journal and write down these thoughts. On paper, ideas became clearer.

The listeners applauded Abel. Nina clapped, a rush of emotions surging through her body. The words echoed her own journey.

Grace appeared at the door of the storage area, looking from Nina to her husband, smiling. Celia suggested another Frost poem for Abel to read, and he readily complied.

Some customers entered the shop, and Nina had to redirect her attention from the reading. Even while busy, she still caught a few words from the poem Inside My Own, which also fit her situation. It spoke of the elusive endeavor of understanding the inner self.

But what direction would she take to discover who she was? There were so many voices, and her mind was confused. She needed a change of mind. Where had she heard that concept before? Perhaps from her father.

The rest of Nina's day passed uneventfully. The poems stayed on her mind, along with the desire to write in her journal. Grace left earlier with Abel, leaving her to close the shop. The shorter autumn days ushered nightfall in earlier. It was the worst time for Nina, when the ghosts emerged from the dark corners. She closed the cash register and sighed with relief when she remembered she would have supper with Jade, Esther and Parker. He had said that if Nina felt scared, he could pick her up from work. The suggestion was tempting, especially as her heart raced while she fumbled with the shop's door lock. She already dreaded the walk back to the inn. Though it was only three blocks away, for someone plagued by fear, it felt like a long distance in the shadows looming with threats.

Zipping up the black hoodie, her camouflage, Nina quickened her pace. The street was still bustling. Some stores remained open, and the restaurants were filling with customers. Nina strode to the end of Main Street. The unsettling sensation of being watched never left her. She quickened her steps at the corner of the inn, heart pounding. She finally breathed a sigh of relief after closing the inn's door.

"Nina, I was waiting for you. I have math homework." Jade burst into the room, notebooks clutched in her hands, the ponytail swinging and the read ribbon fluttering with her hair.

"Jade, give Nina some space." Esther, who was working on her iPad, spoke without taking her eyes off the screen.

"Aaaaah!" Jade stomped off towards the reading nook.

Nina followed her and found the girl sitting on the floor by the coffee table, spreading out her school supplies. "Jade, I need a few minutes to freshen up. Be right back, okay?"

Jade looked up at Nina. "Are you going to wear your new dress?"

"How do you know I bought a dress?"

"Parker told me." She nibbled the tip of her pencil eraser.

In what context would he have mentioned her new clothes to his niece? "I'm comfy in these clothes." She unzipped the dark hoodie and looked at her cheap sneakers.

Jade pouted. "I'll show you my clothes later." She looked down at Nina's feet. "Didn't you like the shoelace I gave you?"

"I didn't have time to change them."

"Jade," her mother called.

Nina laughed. "I'll be right back." Passing by the front desk, she winked at Esther.

In her room, she pulled the glass figurines from the backpack, unwrapped them and arranged them with pride on the dresser. She took a quick shower and got dressed. Jade would be disappointed with the jeans and beige sweater. Perhaps she should pick up a brighter color sweater from the new arrivals at the shop.

Nina smoothed her curly hair and applied lotion to her face and hands. A hint of rose lipstick highlighted her lips, which were returning to their natural size and shape as the fillers wore off. The apples of her cheeks looked more like Nina's and no longer like Catarina's, the monster-doctor's creation.

As she looked at her reflection in the mirror, Nina examined her figure. Her curves were rounder, but if she had gained weight, it was barely noticeable. And she didn't care. The scale was a relic of the past, not present anywhere in Nina's new life in Grace Harbor. Free from Anderson's scrutiny, she had developed a healthier relationship with food. The intense craving for croissants had faded. She now enjoyed her meals, savoring each dish and stopping when she felt satisfied.

Retrieving her journal from the backpack, she returned to the reading nook. Jade was bent over a sheet filled with math exercises. They worked on the addition and subtraction, with Nina guiding the girl when necessary. After a while, each focused on their own tasks. Nina settled on the shell-shaped chair and wrote some thoughts in the journal about her interpretation of Robert Frost's poems. Everything made so much sense.

Change of mind, she wrote and doodled around the phrase. The term sparked a memory. Leaving the journal on the big chair, she went to the bookshelf, under Jade's watchful eyes. She ran her fingers along the spines of the books, reading the titles. She stopped at the one she was looking for: the Bible. Settling back into the chair, she scanned the index. Following her finger on the words and expressions in alphabetical order, she stopped at 'mind.' She read the references. Renewal of the mind. Nina made a note in her journal. Her mind was a mess. She had lived lies for far too long. She considered that the mind needed a detox just like the body. Nina knew how to do the body detox. Anderson had forced her to do that a few times a month, with horrible teas and fasting, but a mind detox was more complicated.

"What are you looking up?" Jade crawled on her knees to Nina's feet, resting her arms on the chair.

"How to change our thoughts." Nina lowered the Bible and looked at the girl.

The girl's eyes sparkled. "You just need to think about good things. That's what my mom and Parker say when I'm scared. Did you know God talks to us about good thoughts?"

"I see it here." Nina pointed to a passage in the Bible.

"Parker said we all have bad thoughts, but it's important to have good thoughts. We are happier."

"I agree." Nina rested her hands on the open Bible, feeling the fine pages.

"When I ran away from you at the pier, Parker told me I need to remember to be obedient. Being disobedient brings sadness to our lives. That's what my mom says. That's why my dad left. He didn't obey what God says." Jade pressed her lips and squinted her eyes as if she were trying hard to concentrate.

Nina stared at the girl's round face, her heart compressing. "I'm sorry he left. It must be hard for you."

"I never met him. My mom said he left when he found out I was special. If I'm special, why did he leave?"

Nina's tears burned her eyes and threatened to spill over. She sniffed, holding them back. "It's hard to know why some people do what they do."

"But Parker came to live with my mom to take care of me. I don't need my dad 'cause I have my uncle."

Nina wanted to sink into the soft chair and hide her face in shame. Here was a little girl who understood the deep questions of life much better than Nina, a grown woman who barely knew who she was. She scooted to one side of the chair and patted the place beside her, inviting Jade to sit. The girl jumped to her side. She rested her head on Nina's shoulder.

"I love you, Nina." Her voice was soft and tender.

Nina's tears rolled down freely. "I love you, Jade."

"Want to know something?" Jade spoke quietly, her head nestled on Nina's shoulder.

"What is it?" She wiped away her tears.

"Parker always reads to me that love is patient and kind. It's in the Bible. He said we should say 'I love you' to those who make us feel special. You are patient with me. You make me feel special."

The warm tears returned, tears that felt different from the ones Nina had shed while in captivity. They were now a blend of tenderness and warmth, tracing soft paths down her cheeks. Words escaped her, leaving her mind in a haze. Even if they had come to her, they would have fallen short of capturing the torrent of emotions in her chest. How could she possibly respond to such a profound declaration of pure love?

Nina had come to Grace Harbor burdened by anger, humiliation, betrayal and scorn. Yet, in a short time, she found herself wrapped in care, affection and love. The love came from a girl who saw the world through a unique lens. With her innocent heart, Jade voiced the truths that skeptical souls like Nina often kept hidden, afraid of being hurt. After all, love required surrender and vulnerability, accepting the risk of disappointment and pain.

This moment felt like another fork in her journey. The well-trodden path was one of self-protection, shielded by the armor of past hurt. The less traveled road was the one Jade was gently guiding her toward—the path of embracing love despite its risks.

Nina seemed to pause at this crossroads, weighing both options. The warmth of Jade's presence and the sincerity of her words made her reconsider her choice, contemplate taking the less traveled road of loving—and maybe even being loved—despite the risks.

Grace Harbor. Where grace was the anchor that steadied her soul. A serene refuge for her tired spirit.

Was it possible for God to transform not just her mind, but also her heart, through Jade? As Nina felt the softness of the girl's hair against her face, hope blossomed, allowing her to believe that such a transformation was possible.

CHAPTER 18

"Turn your head to the other side now." Jade ran the brush through Nina's hair and styled another pigtail. "I'm going to tie this yellow frilly clip in." She hummed something about ocean waves while working on the hairstyle.

Nina, seated in Jade's pink vanity chair, looked at herself in the mirror. The other pigtail was tied with a red scrunchy. According to Jade, Nina needed some color in her clothes and accessories, like, right now! Nina had laughed at the girl's unfiltered bluntness.

"You look great." Jade's gaze met Nina's in the mirror.

Half an hour earlier in the inn's reading nook, Nina and Jade had finished the math homework after spending some time enjoying each other's company and affection while seated in the big chair. Jade had begged her mother to let her play salon with Nina while she and Parker prepared supper.

The smell of food wafted through Jade's bedroom as Nina enjoyed their playtime. Louis, her hairdresser, would be horrified by the childish hairstyle Jade had created. Anderson would be furious if he saw his wife's hair styled with glittery unicorn clips and fluttering butterfly clips.

"All done. Now we just need makeup." Jade put down the hairbrush and opened a colorful box with lipsticks and eyeshadows.

"Wow, I'm beautiful." Nina laughed and complied when Jade told her to close her eyes.

"I'm going to use blue eyeshadow. Blue is my favorite color."

Nina held her laughter and let Jade apply the foam brush to her eyelids. When she opened her eyes, the eyelids were smeared with blue. "That's all?"

"The lipstick. You can choose." She pushed the box closer to Nina.

"I think...the pink one."

"It's my favorite." Jade took the lipstick and applied it to Nina's lips, smudging the corners and her teeth.

Esther called from the hallway, announcing supper was served.

Nina assessed her makeup and hair. "Shall we go?" She got up.

"Just need one last thing. Take off that dull jacket." She skipped over her bed and opened the sliding door of the closet, pulling out a tote bag. From inside, she took out a scarf in rainbow colors. "Just wrap it around your neck."

Nina tied the scarf and looked at herself in the mirror one more time. She hoped Esther and Parker were ready for the surprise. Jade took Nina's hand and pulled her into the kitchen. Her mother and uncle paused, each holding a serving dish, and looked at Nina. Esther shook her head, and Parker circled around the guest, examining the result of their playtime.

"Definitely not lacking in color and texture, that's for sure." He winked at Nina.

She picked up on the comment. "Jade, your uncle needs some tips, too. He only wears dark clothes."

Parker laughed and placed the serving dish on the round table next to others. "No way. I'm fine." He gestured with his hand at his dark pants and gray shirt.

Besides the delicious food, dinner was filled with laughter. Jade and Parker began a session of made-up names for each other while Esther watched the playful exchange as she ate. Nina was included in the game and received several nicknames: Curly, Painted Face, and Ms. Pigtails. For someone who didn't know the meaning of her own name until meeting Jade, Nina now had several. And she loved the banter and each nickname.

For all she cared, she could sign her name Curly Adams if that meant never going back to Catarina Phillips.

After dessert, Jade's energy waned, and she grew irritable. The smallest things annoyed her, like when she couldn't cut the meat or wouldn't be allowed to drink her third glass of iced tea. Esther sent Jade to her room to get ready for bed. The girl stomped her foot, and Parker soon followed her. Esther confided in Nina that Jade got very upset and threw some crying fits when she was tired.

"Parker is more patient than I am." Esther started clearing the table while Nina helped.

"She always seems so cheerful." Nina loaded the dishes into the dishwasher.

"Usually, but when she's tired or upset, watch out."

The two women tidied up the kitchen and sat at the table with a cup of tea. Nina could hear Jade's whining and Parker's firm voice coming from the hallway.

When the girl calmed down, Esther leaned back in her chair with a sigh. "I don't know what I would do without Parker."

"He cares a lot for Jade." Nina turned the mug in her hands, feeling its warmth.

"He's the father she never had. When Jade was born and the doctor said she had Down syndrome, Seth fell apart. He didn't know how to handle the news. A year later, he left home. I was alone with Jade. She doesn't have any recollection of him. At the time, Parker managed the other inn and started coming here more often to help me with the work. He fell in love with his niece. He was twenty at the time, juggling work and online business classes. My brother took on so much responsibility from an early age, but he never complained. Jade became his driving force." Esther sighed and went on, "Sometimes I feel guilty that he hasn't started his own family. He was engaged, but his fiancée couldn't handle his devotion to Jade, so they broke up. He dated someone else after that, but her plans didn't fit with his commitment to his niece. I keep telling him Jade's eleven now and needs less care, but he's as stubborn as ever."

Nina could hear Parker's voice and Jade's laughter. "She's captivating." She grabbed a paper napkin and dabbed at her teary eyes, smudging the blue eyeshadow onto the tissue. "I've learned so much from Jade."

Esther smiled. "She likes you a lot. I've never seen anything like it."

Nina cocked her head. "How's that?"

"She doesn't trust others easily, except for Grace and Abel."

Nina was surprised. What had the little girl seen in her to feel so at ease? "In that case, I feel even more honored to have her trust."

Esther drank the rest of her tea and pushed her cup to the side. "Nina, I don't want to be intrusive, but why did you choose Grace Harbor to live?"

Nina dropped her gaze, feeling it wasn't fair for Esther to open up her life without knowing more about her guest. She looked up. "I came from a tough situation and decided it was time for a change." She then shared the serendipitous meeting with Grace. "An interesting coincidence." The moment Nina uttered that, she rephrased it in her mind. A blessing.

Esther smoothed the tablecloth with her hand. "I don't see it as a coincidence. Grace Harbor is a special place—here we piece together the fragments of broken hearts."

Nina glanced sideways and saw Parker standing in the doorway. How much had he overheard of their conversation? Esther stood up and turned on the electric kettle. She prepared tea for her brother and gestured for him to sit.

"Jade is asleep." He took the mug Esther offered him. "She was too excited playing salon with Nina."

Nina ran her hand through her hair and removed the clips and scrunchies, letting the pigtails fall. "The magic is fading." She laughed and tried to smooth out her curls. "I have so much fun with my new friend."

Parker gazed at her. "She just told me you're the best friend she's ever had."

Nina pressed the blue-stained napkin to her eyes. She told them about the tender moment she had shared with Jade earlier.

Esther rubbed her moist eyes. "Thank you for everything, Nina."

"I don't do it out of obligation. Jade has been a great inspiration to me."

The hum of the dishwasher filled the moment of silence. They sipped their tea, each lost in their own reflections.

A moment passed, and Esther broke the silence, her voice soft, but steady. "Is this change you talked about the right decision?"

Escape a sadistic husband? If only Esther and Parker knew. "The only decision. I took longer than I should have to muster the courage."

Esther nodded, and Parker leaned back in his chair, looking at Nina as if he had an infinity of questions to ask.

"Whatever you need, we're here to support you," he said.

What if Anderson showed up here and exposed who she really was? What would the siblings think? Nina offered them a weary smile and stood up. "I've taken too much of your hospitality. Next time, I'll leave earlier. And since I'll be having supper here frequently, I'd like to cook, too. This way, you both have more time to get things done at the inn."

Esther got up. "Oh, don't you worry. Parker is the one who cooks most of the time. Like today."

Nina looked at him. "The lasagna was wonderful."

He smiled with both his lips and his eyes. "I accept the compliment."

"You should," she replied, heading toward the living room.

"Good night, Nina. I'm going to check on Jade." Esther hugged her and disappeared into the hallway.

Nina looked around. "I left my cell phone in Jade's room."

Parker went over to the coffee table and grabbed the phone. "I brought it here." His fingers brushed hers. "I'll walk you to the inn. I have a few things to sort out in the office before closing."

They walked out and made their way to the inn's rear entrance. Parker unlocked it and let Nina in first.

"Thank you for the lovely time," she said.

"Next time, you don't need to put on all that makeup." He smiled.

Nina playfully hit his strong arm. "You don't need to tell a woman how to do her makeup."

Parker let out a laugh. "True, Ms. Pigtails."

"Watch out, you silly uncle." Nina burst into laughter, a joyous sound she hardly recognized as hers, but that flowed like a stream of refreshing water.

Parker laughed along, then took a breath. "I see you've caught the Baek family's silliness virus."

"I think I have, and I hope there's no cure."

"There isn't." Parker made a funny face with crossed eyes.

CHAPTER 19

After a hectic morning at the shop, Nina rushed to Beth's Bistro for a sandwich. She looked around as she nibbled on the egg salad on rye. Most of the faces were already familiar. But who had paid for her meal two days ago, and why? Had it been a gesture of goodwill or something more unsettling?

Nina tapped her fingers on the edge of the round table. The hum of conversations and clinking of silverware seemed distant. She mustered all her courage to approach Beth, who had just served coffee to a tall woman in a dark blue work coverall. Nina waited behind the woman until she thanked Beth and left. She smiled nervously at the bistro owner.

"How did you like the egg salad?" The woman with dyed blond hair wiped the counter.

"Delicious as always." Nina bit her lower lip. She cleared her throat. "Two days ago, someone paid my bill. Simone didn't know who it was and said you might know."

Beth tapped her long nails on the glass countertop. "Of course. It was Silvia."

A sense of relief washed over Nina. She didn't know who Silvia was, but the generous gesture reflected the spirit of Grace Harbor. "Who's she?"

"The owner of the candy shop on the boardwalk." Beth waved to one attendant and pointed to a table in the back where a couple had just sat down.

"Did she say why she did that?"

"No. She just paid her bill and yours and left."

"Thank you."

Nina returned to work, pondering why a stranger paid her bill. Something felt off despite her relief.

As she got busy with the customers that afternoon, she considered going to the candy shop after closing Love at Second Sight. By then, darkness would have set in. Since fleeing home, every shadow seemed to hold a threat. She glanced at the clock, her impatience growing with each passing minute. A mix of curiosity and apprehension stirred within her. Maybe she could call Parker. He had offered to pick her up if she needed. Well, picking her up to go back to the inn was one thing. Embarking on a mission to the boardwalk to investigate the mystery of the bill was another. She didn't want to burden him with her fears, especially after the wonderful night they had shared with Esther and Jade. She couldn't bring herself to spoil that warmth with her own troubles.

Grace returned to the shop before closing time, after taking the day off to see doctors with Abel.

"How's Abel?" Nina put on her hoodie and grabbed the backpack from a compartment under the counter.

"He's a bit more forgetful, but that's part of the disease's progression. Other than that, he's in good health; heart, lungs and other organs that bother older people like us." Grace smiled and opened a drawer behind the counter.

Nina nodded with sympathy. "You know where to find me if you need any help."

"Thank you for everything and for keeping your commitment." Grace lightly tapped Nina's hand.

Nina smiled. Working at the shop had become more than just an obligation to that commitment. She enjoyed the daily interaction with the people of Grace Harbor who wandered through the door. They shared slices of their lives, and Nina could see her own struggles in a different light. Working at Love at Second Sight gave her purpose. She didn't dread waking up in the morning just to play the role scripted by Anderson. Her life was unscripted. Despite the uncertainties and concerns, Nina preferred this kind of life. The comforting sounds of the inn, the soothing murmur of the waves carried by the morning breeze, the inviting smells of breakfast, all intensified the connection she felt with the town and those around her. And the connection with the Nina she was discovering.

"Thank you for everything." Nina waved Grace goodbye and headed for the door. She pulled it open and froze on the threshold, the bell chiming.

The sun dipped below the horizon, painting the sky purple and dark blue. Nighttime was descending fast. Nina's heart quickened. She had to make it to the boardwalk, but the hair on her arms prickled as she felt a presence, eyes following her.

"Is something wrong?" Grace asked from the counter.

Nina looked over her shoulder. The shop's warm interior seemed miles away. She took a few deep breaths. "No, no." She tried to reassure herself with the emphatic answer, but the apprehension crawled under her skin.

"If you wait, I can walk with you to the corner. I just need to close the register." Grace's voice sounded muffled.

Nina stepped back into the shop and closed the door, leaving the threat outside. She looked at Grace and around at the familiar place. "I'm making a phone call." She lingered toward the reading nook and tapped on the number from her short contact list.

Her senses relaxed when she heard the deep voice. "Hi, Parker. Sorry to bother you, but I need company to go to the boardwalk."

"What's at the boardwalk?" he asked with a concerned tone.

Nina briefly explained her conversation with Beth at the Bistro.

"Be at the shop in ten minutes."

"Is everything alright, dear?" Grace asked from the back of the shop.

"Yes. I'll stick around for a few minutes."

Grace continued her work at the register, focussed on the task. Nina ran her fingers over the spine of the books on the shelves, as if searching for a specific one. Minutes later, Parker entered the shop, the bell chiming softly.

Nina walked toward him under Grace's curious gaze. Parker greeted the older woman and asked about Abel. They chatted before he and Nina left the shop.

"Why would Silvia pay for your meal?" Parker asked.

They walked side by side, arms brushing now and then.

"I have no idea, but it's weird." Nina glanced around. All she saw were familiar faces.

They crossed the street, making their way toward the beach. The sky had deepened into inky black, erasing the vestiges of twilight. A brisk wind swept in from the sea, carrying the scent of salt. The murmur of the waves grew louder. Nina and Parker stepped onto the boardwalk toward the candy shop. Inside, a woman with brown hair tied in a loose bun prepared cotton candy for two teenage girls. Nina inhaled the sweet smell and watched as the fluffy blue cloud grew on the spinning head of the machine. She couldn't help but compare the airy confection to her life with Anderson—all fluff and no substance.

Chatting and giggling, the girls soon left with their cotton candy. The woman smiled at Parker and Nina while she wiped the cotton candy machine. The metal name tag on her uniform read Silvia. She and Parker greeted each other.

Nina approached the counter. "Hi, I'm Nina."

"Blue cotton candy, right?" Silvia rubbed the rag on her finger as she walked to the counter.

"You remember me?"

"You were here with Jade." Silvia leaned against the counter.

Parker nodded. "Beth said you paid for Nina's meal two days ago. We're curious why."

Silvia rested her hands on the glass counter. "I was in line to buy coffee when a man behind me said he wanted to pay for it. I asked him why, and he said he had promised his grandfather he'd be kind to a stranger once a week. An act of kindness. I thought the story was strange, but I accepted it, and he gave me some cash. It was more than the cost of a cup of coffee. I was returning him the extra cash, but he refused to take it back. Said I should pay for your meal. He pointed at you, Nina."

Nina felt the grip of fear on her shoulders. "What did he look like?"

"Middle-aged and balding. He was about my height and chubby."

"Did you see him again after that?" Parker asked.

"Nope. I did what he asked, then he vanished. Never saw him again."

Parker thanked Silvia and gently pulled Nina outside. She was trembling. The oppressive darkness seemed to swallow them whole. Parker wrapped his arm around Nina's waist, drawing her close as they made their way back to the inn. Nina felt unsteady, as though she were on ice for the first time.

At the inn, Esther was helping a customer but cast a worried glance at Nina. Parker motioned for his sister to wait, and guided Nina to the reading room.

"Sit down," he said, placing a supportive hand on her arm.

Nina sank into the chair, her shoulders slumping with the weight of her emotions. "I feel like I'm losing my mind."

Parker pulled another chair, facing her. "Do you want to talk about it? Sharing the burden makes it bearable."

Nina met his gaze, noting the concern in his eyes. "My burden is too heavy to be shared."

"I'm strong." He winked and patted his shoulders.

Nina smiled faintly. "My life—the last six years have been so painful."

His expression turned serious, concern spreading over the high cheekbones and strong jawline. "Painful how?"

Nina closed her eyes and took a deep breath. Parker had done so much for her already. He deserved to know at least a brief version of her story. "I went through—"

Jade pranced into the reading room with her notebooks. "Nina, I have math homework again. Can you help me?" Her bright eyes looked at Nina and Parker. Her innocent mind was oblivious to the heavy atmosphere.

Esther stormed into the room. "I'll help you. Come with me."

"Mom, Nina knows the lesson." She pouted.

Parker stood up and took Jade's hands. "My precious pebble, Nina is not feeling good. After supper, we can play a game. How about it?"

"Dominoes?" Jade's carefree tone was a stark contrast to the gravity of the conversation that was about to happen.

"Dominoes it is," Parker said.

Jade looked at Nina. "Don't get sick, okay?"

Nina nodded, eyes stinging. "Promise."

Esther and Jade left the reading room, and a couple in their forties entered. Parker greeted them and extended his hand to Nina. "Come with me."

He guided Nina through the moonlit backyard. The pine scent wafted in the crisp air as they neared the cottage. Parker opened the front door. A soft, golden light from two lamps spilled out and welcomed Nina. The Baek's home always radiated a sense of warmth.

Parker gestured to the leather sofa. "Please, have a seat." His tone was reassuring. "Something to drink, tea, water?"

Nina shook her head, fingers twisting in her lap. She glanced around the warmly lit room, trying to calm the turmoil in her chest. "I don't know where to start."

Parker sat at the other end of the sofa, his body turned toward Nina. "Why is your past painful?"

Nina lowered her head. She wouldn't have the courage to tell her story while facing someone, anyone. "I'm married. I ran away from my husband." The words spilled out in a whisper.

The burning logs in the fireplace crackled, the shadows of the flames dancing in the room.

"Nina, look at me." His voice was soft, but intense. She raised her head, her eyes heavy. Parker leaned closer to her, but at a safe distance. "This is a safe place."

She nodded. She felt safe. "Anderson. He destroyed who I was."

He shifted in his seat. "Was he violent?"

Nina furrowed her brow and clenched her hands. "Not that kind of violence. But, yes, he was violent."

"I am so sorry, Nina." His eyes met hers, filled with genuine concern.

"Anderson wanted to shape me into his idea of a perfect woman. He's a plastic surgeon. The more he poked and altered me, the farther I slipped away from his standard. I ended up becoming a monster, a sick soul. I hated what I saw in the mirror, hated myself for allowing him to change me. I was a corpse in pretty dresses, in a big house—a zombie." She clutched her curly hair, her hands trembled, her lips quivered.

She told Parker details about her relationship with Anderson—the pressures, demands, and expectations. She described her meticulous routine of cooking, entertaining guests and attending fancy events. Her urge to scream was overwhelming. Her situation had spiraled into such absurdity that it was hard to believe she had even been in it. How had she allowed all that to happen? How had she endured years of emotional abuse, threats and manipulation? Why had she ignored her father's concern? Nina stared at Parker, her heart pounding. What would he think of her? Weak? Pathetic? A victim of her own stupidity? The thoughts twisted in her mind.

He leaned in, his gaze filled with tenderness. "Part of your burden is now mine."

Nina widened her eyes. "I'm sorry. That wasn't my intention. That's why I told you—"

He shook his head. "That's not what I mean. This is your story, your pain. Only you know how it feels. What I'm saying is that from now on, I'll be here for you. I can't erase any of this, though I'd give anything to do it. I understand it will take time to heal and restore your sense of self. Only God can truly heal that part of you, but I promise to stand by your side. I believe every word you've shared with me. I sense there's so much more you've kept to yourself. It must be painful to put these things in words. But God knows. I believe healing and hope are possible."

"There are things that don't heal, Parker." She gasped.

"I understand what you mean. Some things are too terrible, too painful for us to believe there is healing. But I believe there's healing in the form of peace that surpasses all understanding. We can't produce that. It comes from above."

Nina considered his words. She thought of Esther and Jade, and how their husband and father had discarded them like a used piece of toilet paper. Yet, they knew peace. Would Nina ever know this peace that surpassed understanding? Why and how would Parker be part of her journey? "I'm still a married woman."

"I wouldn't do anything differently if you were single or a widow. What I see is a beautiful person who is hurt, who confided something very painful to me. From now on, I have a responsibility to help."

She frowned. "That's not your responsibility."

"Those blessed much find it in their hearts to give much."

Grace had said that when Nina first met her. "I don't understand."

Parker moved closer to Nina. "You see, I received the great gift of raising my niece. Jade is my gift, my precious pebble. How can I not give back after receiving so much?"

Nina let out a sob and allowed the tears to fall. Parker reached for the side table and grabbed a box of tissues. She took a handful and wiped her eyes.

What was it about Grace Harbor that made her let her guard down? If only she could free herself from the grip of fear, she wouldn't mind spending all her days in this place where the less-traveled path had brought her.

CHAPTER 20

The three untouched cups of coffee rested on the polished coffee table. The golden flickering light from the fireplace bathed Nina and Esther, both in silence. Esther, hugging a throw pillow, had her head tilted to the side, as if it weighed a lot. Nina twisted the hem of her sweater. She looked at the untouched coffee cups and thought how little of the spaghetti she had eaten with the brother and sister an hour ago. Anxiety tightened her stomach. She wasn't nervous about opening a painful chapter of her life with Parker, and later with Esther. The icy feeling in her spine came from having to go back to her empty bedroom at the inn. By opening the wounds, her fear had intensified.

Parker returned to the living room and sat on the sofa next to Nina. "Jade is asleep now. She was worried about you, Nina. Wanted to know what's wrong."

Esther caressed the pillow as if caressing a child's head. "She is very sensitive to changes in the behavior of the people she loves."

Nina tightened her grip, her fingers turning white. "I'm so sorry. I should never have brought my problem into your home."

Esther stood up and threw the pillow on the sofa. She knelt in front of Nina and took her hands. "Don't say that. In our family, we are each other's refuge."

"Exactly. I'm not family."

"That's not true." Parker shifted his body closer to Nina. He softened his expression. "Jade considers you an aunt or a big sister. Trust me—she isn't that clingy with anyone."

Esther squeezed Nina's hand and sat on the edge of the coffee table. "The other day, she asked me if she could move to the room next to yours. She said she was a grown-up now and needed her own space." She rolled her eyes.

Nina rubbed her forehead and smiled. "I've always wanted a sister."

"Then let's stop this talk about not being part of the family." Parker stood up, took the three cups of coffee, and carried them to the kitchen area. Soon he returned with three bottles of water. "If we're truly family, I'm in a position to say Nina hasn't eaten much at suppertime. You must be starving. Should I make you something—toast, an omelette?"

Nina's chin quivered. Never, in the last six years, had she been treated with this much consideration and care. Her role had been to ensure that the powerful Dr. Anderson Phillips always looked good. She grabbed the bottle from Parker's hand. "I don't think I could eat right now."

"Then I'll prepare a snack bag in case you get hungry during the night." He went back to the kitchen.

Esther sat on the sofa beside Nina. "You look shaken. Would you like to spend the night here?"

Nina let out a long, deep sigh. "I have no more pride left today. Yes, I'd love that."

"Jade will do cartwheels when she wakes up and sees you next to her. Don't be surprised if she knocks you over." Esther stood up. "I'll make the bed."

Parker returned with a paper bag and handed it to Nina. "Muffins, cheese strings—"

Nina peeked inside the bag. "I'm sort of hungry now." She grabbed a blueberry muffin and took a hearty bite.

"Now we're talking." Parker sat beside Nina.

As the blueberries exploded in her mouth, she thought about how Anderson controlled her meals and portions. She felt like an obese dog only allowed rationed meals. "What else is in here?"

Parker laughed. "A small container with green grapes. Hope you like grapes."

She pulled the plastic container and opened the lid. "Green, yellow, purple, any color."

Parker laughed louder.

Esther returned to the room. "Your bed is ready."

Parker looked at his sister with raised eyebrows. Nina closed the container and put it back into the bag. "It's your fault if I'm exploiting the goodwill of the family."

"Exploit us at your leisure." Parker bowed with theatrical flair.

Under the covers that smelled of summer breeze fabric softener, Nina let her head sink into the soft pillows. She looked at the silhouette of the mountain of blankets on the bed beside hers. The bluish light from the night lamp on the wall, the shadows of Jade's furniture and the sound of doors opening and closing in the hallway wiped all the tension away from her. She hardly knew the Baek family, but the sense of protection and security she felt in that home seemed almost supernatural in its intensity.

***

Nina opened her eyes to find a round face with a radiant smile staring at her. "Good morning, Jade."

In response, the girl lifted Nina's blanket and snuggled underneath it. "Are you going to live with us? You can stay in my room forever. I'll clear out a shelf in my closet for you."

Nina propped herself up on her elbow and ran a hand through her tousled hair. She had slept so deeply that her skin felt wrinkled like the sheets. "I spent the night just this once. I wasn't feeling well yesterday, and your mother invited me to stay here."

"Do you know what day it is today?" Jade turned onto her stomach, resting her chin on her crossed arms.

"Saturday." Nina yawned.

"That's right." She turned her smiling face towards Nina. "It's the best day of the week. Sunday is good too, because I can wear something fancy to church."

"And why is Saturday the best day?"

"Parker takes me to the beach."

"Isn't it chilly to go to the beach?"

Jade sat cross-legged. "We swim when it's hot. When it's colder, we fly kites. Do you know how to fly a kite?"

"No. Is it hard?" Nina leaned against the pillows.

"I can teach you."

"I've got to work until two."

"Parker gotta work, too. We go when he finishes his work on the computer. You can come with us."

"We should ask Parker if I can come."

"Okay." Jade jumped out of bed and ran down the hallway in her pink pajamas, calling out her uncle's name.

Nina laughed at Jade's literal interpretation. She sat on the bed and put on the robe that Esther had lent her, which matched her dark blue nightgown.

Jade returned, pulling Parker by the hand. He rasped on the open door, looking away from Nina, and asked if he could come in.

"Sure." Nina tied the robe's sash.

"Sorry to barge in, but Jade said you were already up." His eyes met hers.

Nina was sure her hair looked like a bird's nest after the long, uninterrupted sleep. But studying Parker's carefree disposition, she relaxed. "I was invited to kite flying. I don't want to intrude."

"You're more than welcome to join us. It's a great day to fly kites. What time do you get off work?" He leaned on the doorjamb, arms crossed, grin on his clean-shaven face.

Jade plopped on her bed, bouncing like popcorn on a pan. "Nina gets off at two. She told me." Jade picked up a teddy bear and hugged it. "It's going to be an awesome day, Teddy!"

"Then we'll plan for three. I have a few errands to run. Be back after lunch," Parker said.

Jade threw the teddy bear up in the air, clapped her hands, and ran down the hallway when her mother called for her.

"Did you sleep well?" Parker unfolded his arm, straightening his back.

"Like a baby on clouds." She glanced at herself in the vanity mirror. Her appearance was not of a baby, but she didn't care. For the first time in ages, Nina felt well rested and ready to discover her purpose in the next chapters of her life.

"You know you can spend the night here whenever you want," Parker said.

Nina stood up. She smoothed out the sheets and fluffed the pillows. Lifting the quilt, she let it drape over the bed. The morning light seeped through the blinds. "I'm already intruding too much." She made Jade's bed with the same fluid motion.

"One thing I've learned from Esther and Jade is that sometimes we need a shoulder to lean on." Parker stepped into the room and picked up a pile of Jade's clothes from the floor. He folded the T-shirts and colorful pants.

Nina sighed and grabbed her clothes from the vanity chair. "My idea of friendship is distorted. I'm still getting used to this new meaning."

Parker placed the folded clothes on the bed. "Esther and Jade have been that shoulder for me."

Nina hugged her clothes and raised an eyebrow. Did Parker need his sister and niece? He seemed so secure in everything. "In what way?" Her curiosity overcame her discretion.

Parker drew the blinds open and leaned against the windowsill, the sun casting a glow on his dark hair. "When I decided to help my sister after Seth left, I had no idea what I was getting into." He let out a sad laugh. "I was young, idealistic, and determined to take care of Jade. It wasn't easy. I knew nothing about babies, let alone atypical babies. Esther tried to convince me to live my life. My resolve was firm, but many times I cried on her shoulder, feeling like a failure."

Nina sat at the edge of Jade's bed, looking up at the face of a man who had no qualms about sharing his weakness. "But you stayed."

Parker sat beside Nina. "Stubbornness. Pride."

"And how was Jade that shoulder for you?" Nina had no doubt the girl's special gifts of simplicity and innocent wisdom.

"She'd notice when I was feeling down, take my hand and tell me I was her hero. Maybe she was projecting the characters from her children's books onto me. Truth is, I felt anything but heroic. I thought of giving up hundreds of times. Everything felt so overwhelming."

Nina ran her hands over the rough fabric of her hoodie in her lap. "But you didn't give up."

"My pride was stronger, I think." His eyes were heavy, faint lines etched into his face.

"Don't you think it was love that made you stay?" Nina was stunned by her own words, she, an abused woman, who had struggled to believe in love.

Parker rubbed his eyes. "Maybe what started as pride, a very selfish feeling, turned into love. God knows all things. He's changed my heart. I'm sure I would have done many things differently, but being with Esther and Jade is my greatest mission."

"Sacred duty." Where had Nina pulled that from? Searching her memory, she recalled that her mother used to say that caring for a child was a sacred duty, a noble task, her noble sacrifice.

With a furrowed brow, he looked at Nina. "What do you mean?"

She shrugged. "I don't even know why that came to my mind. It's your sacrifice, your noble task. As you said, your mission." Purpose!

Parker cocked his head, as if weighing the words carefully. "From this angle, yes. My noble task, even if I did it out of an obligation."

"Commitment?" Wasn't that what Nina had read in the Bible the other day?

His smile brightened the angular face, like the warm sunlight streaming through the window. "Love as in unconditional commitment," he said. "The greatest kind of love. I'm not sure I can love like that."

Jade's shout came from down the hall. "Uncle Parker, Lettuce-Head, come have breakfast."

Nina smiled and stood up, her clothes cradled in her arms. "There's your proof."

Parker followed Nina to the door. "You are wise. And going back to the invitation—spend the night here whenever you want."

"I don't think I'm wise. But thank you for the invitation. I will consider it."

"No pressure. Your decision." He smiled.

"Thank you, Parker. This means a lot to me."

He clapped his hands. "I'll see you later. What's your favorite color?"

Nina looked at the clothes she held and laughed. "Believe me, I like blue. According to Jade, I need more color in my life."

"This time will come, don't you think?"

Nina felt a soothing balm spread through her body. "I hope so."

Jade shouted again, this time calling her uncle Broomstick. Parker excused himself, disappeared down the hallway, calling his niece Talkie Macawley. Nina laughed and ran to the bathroom to change. She declined Esther's invitation for breakfast. She needed to rush to work.

Walking toward Main Street, Nina thought about the conversation she'd had with Parker. What other difficulties had he faced while raising his special niece? Nina knew little about the needs of a child like Jade. She knew little about the needs of any child. She had never thought about having children because Anderson insisted that they'd only get in the way. In hindsight, it was better they never had any. A child in a mess like Nina's would suffer in the chaos they didn't deserve.

Nina interrupted her train of thought as soon as she entered the shop. No point speculating. She had fifteen minutes to get everything ready before opening. There were some items she still needed to put on the shelves. Saturdays were always busy at Love at Second Sight. Customers flocked to the shop, eager for new purchases and a chance to catch up on the week's news. Nina darted back and forth, restocking and tidying up the shelves.

She opened the shop on time despite the rush. Two middle-aged women waited at the door. They greeted Nina and headed straight for the décor section. One of them spoke loudly and laughed at her friend's comments about her grandkids. Nina rearranged the clothes on the rack before heading to the reading nook with a cart full of donated volumes. She shelved the books and hurried back to the counter to help a man who had rushed in to pick out a wedding anniversary gift for his wife. Meanwhile, the two women continued to explore the selection of décor items and exchange stories about their grandkids.

The door opened and closed several times, the bell chiming to greet the customers. Grace called and told Nina that she was arriving later. Abel had had a restless night and was still sleeping. Nina reassured her boss she would manage the work. The two friends finally left with their purchases, which Nina helped carry to their car.

A little before lunchtime, the bustle quieted down. Beth's Bistro and the other restaurants would be full in the next two hours. Nina took the time to organize some boxes in the stockroom. She sorted through the items and separated them by price range.

The doorbell jingled, and Nina stepped out to the counter. A tall, elegant, middle-aged woman walked in carrying a box. The stylish pixie cut framed her beautiful but sad face.

"Good afternoon, welcome to Love at Second Sight." Nina walked over to the woman and helped her set the box down on the counter.

The woman offered a faint smile. The rims of her eyes were red. "I'm donating these books. Abel will appreciate them."

Nina opened the box lid and looked inside. "Thank you. Would you like to leave a note? Abel and Grace might want to know who made the donation."

The woman nodded. Nina tore off a sheet from a notepad and handed it to her. With smooth, elegant strokes, the woman wrote her name: Shirley Elias.

Nina was caught off guard as Shirley started crying, the flow of tears streaming down her face. Grabbing a box of tissues, she offered it to her. Shirley got a handful of tissues with trembling hands. Nina invited the woman to a nearby armchair in the reading nook.

What had broken Shirley's heart? During her time working at the Little Shop of Broken Hearts, Nina had encountered countless sources of anguish—illness, broken relationships, grief, regrets, loneliness. Not even Jade had been spared from pain.

What could be the story behind Shirley's heartbreak? She had come to the right place, much like Nina when she stumbled upon Grace, and her path had taken an unexpected turn.

CHAPTER 21

The cascade of tears continued to stream down Shirley's face. Nina waited, sitting in the armchair facing her. This was the Little Shop of Broken Hearts after all, right? The residents of Grace Harbor seemed to take the name and intention of the shop seriously. Nina had heard countless stories from the many patrons of the place. Sometimes she considered whether it was worth working in a place that attracted so much pain. Wasn't she running away from pain? But what made Grace Harbor a special place was not the tranquility on its surface but the reality of people's experiences. You could only see the true layers of their souls when you understood their afflictions—those silent battles and hidden scars. There, watching Shirley soak several tissues, Nina contemplated her purpose in having gotten a job at Love at Second Sight.

Shirley pressed the tissue to her nose and looked at Nina, her eyes red and swollen. "Please forgive me for taking your time."

Nina glanced at the long, trembling fingers of the silver-haired lady. "Oh, do not worry. The foot traffic at this hour is lighter. Would you like something to drink? Coffee, tea, or water?"

"Maybe a glass of water." Shirley sniffled.

Nina hurried to the corner of the shop that served as a kitchenette and filled a glass with water from a pitcher. She handed Shirley the glass.

Grace walked into the shop with her husband. Abel made a beeline toward the reading nook, settling into one armchair. His stare was distant and unfocused. Nina examined his vacant expression and turned to Grace, who shrugged and nodded, indicating that Abel was not having a good day.

"Thank you very much," Shirley said. "I'm so sorry to cause you trouble. Please, go back to work. I'm fine. Grace needs you." Shirley tossed the small pile of tissues she had accumulated in her lap into the trash can beside her.

"Thank you for the donation." Nina stood up and went over to Grace.

"Did Shirley leave this box?" Grace pointed at the box with books.

Nina picked up the paper with the woman's name. "The books seem to be in great shape."

"I'm surprised she's donating these books. It's no wonder she looks so sad." Grace took the books out of the box, examining each one.

A couple with two young children entered the shop, drawing Nina's attention. As she went over to the family, she couldn't shake her curiosity about Grace's remark regarding Shirley and her donation. Guiding the family through the selection of children's shoes, Nina's gaze kept drifting back to Shirley. The woman shared a few quiet words with Grace before leaving the shop, shoulders sagging.

As the shop buzzed with activity after lunchtime, Nina's memory of Shirley faded. She darted from the cash register to the floor, helping customers while Grace managed the stockroom. Just before closing time, Jade sent a message to Nina from her mom's phone, brimming with excitement about their beach adventure. Nina's reply was short but cheerful, punctuated with several happy-face emojis.

"What's the plan for today?" Grace locked the shop door and changed the sign to 'Closed.' "You deserve a break. It's been a busy day."

"I'm going to fly a kite at the beach with Jade and Parker." Nina arranged the hangers on the rack.

Grace cocked her head. "Parker, huh?"

Nina's face flushed. Was Grace implying there was something between her and Parker? If Grace only knew she was married. Perhaps she should know—Nina owed her coming to Grace Harbor to Grace herself. She walked over to the counter and met her boss's gaze. "It's not like that."

Grace opened the cash register and took out the money, closing the drawer afterward. "There's nothing wrong with that."

"There is. I'm married." Nina braced herself for a look of shock and even reproach from her boss. Instead, Grace squeezed her arm gently.

"Now it all makes sense; you seemed lost and terrified at the station."

Nina looked down and then back to Grace. "I ran away from my husband."

"Violence?"

"The kind that doesn't leave marks."

"Even so, it's violence. No one runs away without a reason."

Nina shared her story with Grace. Repeating her story was emotionally strenuous, but it also gave her a conviction that what she had gone through was abuse. "The problem is," Nina said, her voice tinged with frustration, "I don't know what to do. Am I supposed to live as a fugitive, as if I were the criminal?"

"Have you talked with the authorities?" Grace's expression was heavy.

Nina had heard countless stories of women who reported the abuse but ended up being accused of lying. The narratives were twisted in a way that portrayed the victims as unreliable or unstable. Physical evidence of assault was easier to prove, though even that didn't always lead to justice. But the scars on the soul were invisible and impossible to report. "I don't think it would matter. Anderson is powerful and well-connected. His money and influence speak louder than my pathetic voice."

Grace squeezed Nina's hand. "Things are different now. People take it more seriously."

"That means I have to return to Cleveland, confront Anderson and endure a long process." What would the benefit be? Nina ran her hand through her hair. "I already know the result—more humiliation, pressure and threats."

"Are you going to be tied to a man like that? Listen, dear, I take divorce seriously." Grace looked at her husband, who held an open book but kept his gaze blank toward the window. "I know marriage is for better or worse. I don't mean you should go back to your husband. That would be dangerous, even more so when he must be upset that you left. But hiding indefinitely will only increase your emotional burden."

"What should I do then?" Nina frowned.

"I don't have an answer. So, we pray for one. There are things, dear, that only God can do, things that surpass understanding."

Nina ran her nails along the counter, making an invisible line. "When I ran away, all I wanted was a little peace. That meant staying away from Anderson. I know I'll need to face this situation sooner or later, but I don't know if I'm ready right now."

"I know a lawyer. You can start by talking to her. Take small steps and wait on the Lord to do the big things. How about that?"

"I don't have money for a lawyer." At least, no money that belonged to her.

"Don't worry. If you allow me, I'll schedule the appointment. It won't cost you anything."

Nina's phone vibrated in the back pocket of her jeans. She pulled it out. It was a message from Parker. "I need to think about it, Grace."

The woman squeezed Nina's shoulder. "In the meantime, I'll pray."

"Thank you." She put on her hoodie and grabbed her backpack.

Grace pointed to the rack of shoes against the wall. "You'll need a pair of rain boots. This time of year, the sand is wet."

Nina scanned the rack, stopping at a pair of blue boots with umbrella prints. "I think Jade will approve of this pair."

Grace nodded. "She sure will. Have fun."

Nina said goodbye to Grace and to Abel, who remained gazing vacantly out the window.

***

Three kites danced with grace in the crisp afternoon air, their colorful tails snaking freely. One a deep red, another royal blue and the third sunny yellow, they climbed higher and higher in the blue sky.

Nina wished she could soar like the kites, weightless, free. She could hardly remember a moment so simple, yet so delightful. Perhaps when she was a little girl riding a bike with her parents or playing with her friends—carefree and joyful. How wonderful to find beauty in pieces of colorful paper fluttering in the air. How liberating to feel the wind against her face, to run on damp sand while looking up, and not around in fear.

Jade's purple raincoat and matching boots glistened as she trampled on the damp sand. Three pairs of rain boots left trails of crisscrossing patterns. Jade's laughter blended with the soft roar of the ocean.

Parker shouted some instructions, his voice partially drowned out by the noise of the sea and wind. "... pull the string, Jade."

The kites veered close to each other as Nina, Parker and Jade maneuvered them. A Saint Bernard barked and leaped with enthusiasm, joining the fun. His owner called out repeatedly, but the big dog ignored her until he finally trotted away.

A gust of wind pushed Nina's kite down, and she watched as it began to plummet into the sea. Parker dashed over to her and said, "Turn it around and pull on the line." She followed his instructions, and soon her kite climbed back into the sky. Jade squealed with delight, and Nina echoed her excitement. The fun went on until light raindrops began to fall, forcing Nina and her friends to bring the kites down.

"Better run." Parker said.

Nina and Jade handed their kites to him, and he placed them in a plastic bag. On the way home, Nina offered to make supper and suggested they pick up ingredients for her delicious creamy chicken. They took a detour and walked side by side to the grocery store a block away. When they arrived, Jade grabbed a shopping cart and rolled it into the market. Nina and Paker followed behind.

"I need chicken breast, heavy cream, condiments and greens for a salad." Nina pointed to an aisle.

"I'll get the chicken and greens. You and Jade get the rest." Parker ran his hand through his damp hair and headed toward the meat section.

"Come with me, Jade." Nina pointed to the shelves of condiments. The girl followed, pushing the cart. "I need Dijon mustard. Here." Nina scanned the jars, and a wave of unease rose in her stomach. Horseradish. The thought of Anderson flooded her memory, dissolving part of the afternoon's joy. She shook her head to rid herself of the horrible sensation and grabbed a jar of mustard, placing it in the cart.

Jade pointed to the shelf ahead. "I'll get some olives. I love olives. Green ones." The girl skipped away, leaving the cart behind. Nina kept an eye on her.

Jade stood on her tiptoes, reaching for the jar. Fearing the imminent crash of jars tumbling to the floor, Nina hurried to her. "I'll get it." She pulled the jar and returned to the cart.

A wave of vertigo and nausea engulfed her.

Inside the cart, next to the Dijon mustard, was a jar of horseradish. Nina's heart raced, and her mouth dried. She leaned against a shelf, pushing several jars of mustard, which clanked against each other.

"Nina, what's wrong?" Jade poked her on the ribcage. "You look weird." She puckered her lips, about to cry.

Parker arrived with a package of chicken breasts. "What's going on?" He walked over to Nina and held her by the arm. "You look pale."

With a trembling hand, she pointed to the jar of horseradish in the cart. "That jar... it just appeared in the cart."

"It wasn't me. I wanted the green olives." Jade's voice trailed off, her eyes wide with confusion.

"I don't understand." Parker grabbed the horseradish jar and surveyed it.

"Anderson... he liked this... I hate it. I don't know how this..." Nina pointed to the jar, "appeared in the cart."

"Who is Anderson? Is he mean?" Jade sniffed.

Parker placed his hand on his niece's shoulder. "Someone Nina knows, but that's not important right now. Let's go home."

They paid for their purchase and stepped onto the sidewalk. Nina glanced around, shoulder tense and stomach knotted with anxiety.

Parker switched the bag to the other hand and held Nina by the arm. "We're here with you. Let's get home."

Nina grabbed Jade's hand, seeking the comfort of her soft skin. The girl always brought her a sense of calm, even if she didn't realize it. Jade symbolized a part of Nina's life she hadn't known before—of community, acceptance, protection and purpose. Walking beside Parker, Nina sighed. Although she felt secure with his family, the jar of horseradish hinted at a threat. Anderson wouldn't let her go. His mission had always been to crush her, erase her identity and shatter her dignity.

At the inn, Parker asked Jade to take the groceries to the cottage and wait there. She mumbled a few words that included olives and mean man. On the phone, Esther frowned, a question mark in her expression. Nina shook her head and signaled that she would explain what had happened later.

"I'll take you to your room, so you can change out of those wet clothes. I'll wait outside. Bring what you need to spend the night at the house," Parker said.

They went up the stairs to her room. She turned to him. "I need to take a shower and call my dad. You don't need to wait." Deep down, the last thing Nina wanted was to be alone with the unsettling feeling that Anderson was watching her.

Parker looked over her shoulder and surveyed the room. "I'll be downstairs. If you need anything, message me."

Nina thanked him, entered the room, and closed the door. She opened the bathroom door and craned her neck to survey inside. More relaxed, she took off her wet clothes. She showered and put on dry clothes. She picked up the phone and sent a message to Parker, letting him know she'd finished her shower and was calling her dad.

Take your time. I'm waiting, he replied.

"Dad." Nina clasped the phone and examined Martin's face on the screen. Despite the worry in his eyes, his face looked fuller. The last time they spoke, he mentioned that the doctor had lowered the dose of the depression medication.

"Nina, is everything okay? You look worried."

In a few words, Nina narrated the incident at the market. "Anderson is up to something. I know it. It wasn't a coincidence. No one here knows his taste for horseradish." Nina's heart raced when her father let out a grunt.

He brought a hand to his forehead and massaged it. "You know the man I thought was following me? I asked a friend from the precinct to investigate. He's a detective, just as we suspected."

Nina shivered. "Is he still following you?"

"I haven't seen him for a couple of weeks."

"But that doesn't mean he has given up on following you, Dad. Or maybe there's someone else, someone new."

"I thought about it. The other day, I drove past your old house. I saw a housekeeper leaving and a food delivery car arriving. Anderson is around here."

Nina sat on the edge of the bed. "So, he sent someone to scare me." Could it be the bald man who paid for the meal at the bistro?

Her father leaned closer to the screen, his gaze fixed on Nina. "I'm planning to visit you. In the meantime, be very careful."

Nina shook her head. "Don't come. It's risky."

"After the horseradish incident, it's obvious that Anderson is up to something. But I'll be careful. This friend from the precinct will help me slip out without being tracked. Don't worry."

Nina longed for her father's embrace. "When are you coming?"

"In a few days. I'll let you know. I just need the right moment."

"Okay. Miss you."

"I miss you too, honey." He smiled, but there was sadness in his gaze.

CHAPTER 22

D espite the weight of her heavy heart, Nina prepared the creamy chicken recipe she had promised Esther, Parker and Jade. The incident in the grocery store was put to rest, although Nina could see the concern in Esther's and Parker's eyes. Jade's good mood had returned, and she made Nina smile several times. The rest of the evening was uneventful. After supper, Parker went back to the inn to work, Jade settled with a puzzle, while Nina and Esther drank tea by the fireplace.

The next morning, Nina woke up in Jade's room with a sense of peace. It was comforting to know she wasn't alone. For the first time, she accepted the family's invitation to church. As she walked into the old chapel, she felt like the prodigal daughter returning to her father's house. After six years living in a surreal world of appearances, Nina still sometimes felt like an outsider in the close-knit community of Grace Harbor. While she wasn't naïve enough to believe that relationships there were conflict free, she understood their struggles were part of a greater purpose—strengthening bonds.

"Did you like our church?" Jade asked, holding Nina's hand on the way back to the inn.

"I did. Very much."

Esther and Parker walked behind them, their conversation centered on the inn's affairs. The weak fall sun cast its warmth against the chill of the ocean breeze. Nina's long plaid jacket flapped as they crossed the street toward the inn.

"You can go again any time you want." Jade's almond-shaped eyes looked at Nina as if expecting an answer.

"Thank you. I'd like that."

Jade swung her arm back and forth, pulling Nina along with her. The short walk with family eased some of her worries about being followed. Her father would soon become part of that new circle of friends. He would see with his own eyes that Nina had found the perfect place to mend her broken heart. If only Anderson would leave her alone for good.

Nina had lunch with the family, but by evening, she insisted on sleeping in her own room, despite Jade's protests and Esther's insistence. Parker inspected the room before Nina closed herself in for the night. With her phone tucked under the pillow, she slept soundly.

On Monday, Nina told Grace that she would talk to the lawyer when her father arrived. She needed his insight.

Midweek, Shirley Elias returned to the shop. Nina was opening some boxes with donations in one corner when she saw the woman step in. "Good morning. How can I help you?"

The blue eyes, with soft signs of age, gazed toward the reading nook. "I hope my donation was useful."

"Very much." Nina walked over to Shirley. "The book club members chose one of your books to read next."

"I'm glad. My husband was a college professor. English. My house always had more books than I could ever read." She forced a smile as she looked at Nina. "Would you mind if I sat there for a minute?" Shirley pointed to the reading nook.

"Not at all. That's what we're here for. Would you like some coffee or tea?"

"No, thank you. I'm fine." She walked toward the armchairs and, choosing the one closest to the window, sat down.

The bell at the door chimed, and Silvia, the owner of the candy shop, walked in. She was looking for a cocktail dress. For the next half hour, Nina helped her. Occasionally, she glanced at Shirley, who was reading one book she had donated.

When Silvia left, other customers arrived. Grace stepped in to handle the sales, while Nina carried a cup of tea over to Shirley.

"I thought you might like some chamomile tea." She placed the cup on the round side table.

Shirley lowered the book onto her lap. "Thank you." She sipped the tea. "Grace does a great job here. I never thought I'd soon be one of them."

Nina tilted her head. "One of them?"

"People with broken hearts." She offered a faint smile, her fingers tracing the pattern of the worn fabric of the armchair. "I thought I had everything under control in my life. Even when Rodney died, I believed I'd manage just fine. I was wrong. And here I am."

Nina swallowed hard, the weight of emotions compressing her chest. She listened to Shirley's story about her husband's sudden death of a massive heart attack. Despite inevitable disagreements, their love endured for thirty-six years. She spoke about their grown son, married and living in Scotland.

Nina couldn't help but consider what it would be like to share a life with someone for so long. Even her honeymoon with Anderson was anything but happy. He had shown his true nature on their second day at a beach resort. First, little things like 'Don't eat this; eat that.' Then, inconvenient comments about her body. Back in Cleveland, the demands escalated. Even in times of calm, Nina soon learned, a storm was brewing.

Shirley shared her heart. Nina listened. What could she add? Days earlier in Jade's room, Parker had talked about the importance of offering a shoulder. That was what she could provide.

After some time, Shirley thanked Nina for listening to her and left, gratitude in her eyes. Throughout the day, Nina couldn't shake the weight of Shirley's heartbreak. The deep yearning to reunite with her father and the Baek family grew. When her workday ended, she hurried to the inn and called Martin, then dashed to the cottage, heart racing with anticipation.

***

The train emerged around the bend through a tunnel of autumn trees. It slowed down and released a toot that echoed across the platform. Craning her neck to peep through the train's many windows, Nina strolled along the familiar station that had welcomed her nearly five months ago in a twist of fate that changed her life. Who could have foreseen the changes that had unfolded in such a short time? How could she have imagined a quirky little shop and a special girl would open her eyes to a new world?

Some children broke free from their parents and ran along the platform, waving to relatives or friends, eager for a hug. The train screeched to a halt, and the passengers began to get off. Some met their loved ones while others walked to the parking lot or the taxi stand. Nina had arrived in Grace Harbor with Grace, feeling the weight of loneliness. Soon she mirrored Grace's friendly hellos to passersby in a town that had become her home. The only thing that Nina craved was the peace of mind to wander the streets without the haunting fear of the dark.

The great news was that her dad was coming to her. Martin had sent a message detailing how his police friend would drive him to the station in the neighboring city. He assured his daughter that they had taken every precaution to avoid being followed. It didn't ease her anxiety much because someone was watching her. Maybe not Anderson himself, but someone he'd sent.

Nina spotted her father stepping out of the second car and ran to him. They hugged and whispered words of relief. In his embrace, Nina felt his arms were stronger, much like he had been before. His eyes sparkled as they talked about the train ride and his first impression of Grace Harbor. She felt an overwhelming urge to care for her father, to give back what she had received as a shy little girl and an insecure teenager.

Esther had already prepared the room next to Nina's for Martin. Jade had been ecstatic when Nina told her she was leaving for the station to meet her dad, and the girl had thrown a fit when her mother didn't allow her to go with Nina. Esther's explanation that father and daughter needed to meet alone had been in vain. Parker had intervened and taken his niece to her room. Nina had heard a scolding, but soon they were exchanging funny nicknames. She enjoyed the dynamic of her friends' home, with Jade's outbursts, Parker's sense of humor and Esther's patience. It was a delightful normality, a genuine environment of mistakes and successes. Nina was eager to share details with her father about her new family.

"So, this is Grace Harbor." Martin looked around while pulling the suitcase with one hand and holding his daughter's shoulders with the other.

Nina felt a sudden pride for the small town. "Yes, Dad. As the name says, it really is the harbor of grace."

They walked along the sidewalk toward the inn. Nina greeted some passersby.

Her father looked at her with interest. "I see you've made some friends."

"My work at the shop gives me lots of time to meet people with broken hearts." She laughed at her father's expression and told him about Love at Second Sight, and why it was known as the Little Shop of Broken Hearts.

"When you told me you worked in a shop, I didn't think it was something so special."

They chatted about the shop as they approached the inn. Martin was greeted by Jade, who was waiting at the gate. As if they were already family, the girl took his hand and pulled him inside, chattering about his room.

"Jade couldn't wait to meet you." Esther introduced herself to Martin Adams.

Martin shook Esther's hand with a broad smile on his face. "Glad I'm here."

"Welcome to Grace Harbor. I hope you enjoy your stay here." Esther handed the key to the new guest.

"If my daughter likes it, I like it, too. Thank you for what you've done for her."

Jade tugged at the hem of Martin's coat. "Nina is part of our family. You can be, too."

He bent down to the girl's level. "Can I be your uncle?"

Jade put her index finger to her chin and thought. "You're old. Your hair is white. You can be my grandfather."

Esther stepped out from behind the counter. "Jade, that's not very polite."

Martin burst out laughing. "Fair enough," he said to Jade. "I'll be your grandfather, then."

Esther slung her arm around Jade's shoulder. "My daughter is impossible."

"Parker is my uncle, and he's old, but not that old," Jade said, clearly enjoying the conversation.

"Me, old?" Parker entered the reception and extended his hand to the newcomer, introducing himself. He ruffled his niece's hair. "Precious pebble, no comments about age, remember?"

Jade crossed her arms and pouted. "But I also want to tell Grampa Adams that I'm almost twelve."

The adults laughed, and the girl joined in. Nina wished that moment could stretch on longer. She was welcome to be herself with them. With her father's arrival, she knew more pieces of her life would fall into place.

Grace had given her the day off, so Nina showed Martin to his room. She waited in her room while her father settled in and took a shower. In the meantime, she opened her journal and wrote more reflections, as she did every day. As Nina tucked the journal into the dresser drawer, her hand grazed the envelope containing the documents she had discovered in the closet and in Anderson's study. She needed to show them to her dad. A few times, Nina had overheard her husband talk on the phone. Sometimes his tone of voice was intimate, almost sensual. Nina had suspected an affair. Other times, Anderson was angry, his words harsh and frustrated. She never found out who he was talking to. Same person, different people? Each of these conversations confirmed Nina was not part of Anderson's life. She was a puppet.

She opened the door when her father knocked. She motioned for him to sit in the chair and handed him the papers. "I found this at home before I ran away. What do you think they mean?"

Martin scrutinized the material with the sharp gaze of someone used to analyzing evidence. "Where did you find them?"

"The paper with the numbers and Dutra's name was in the closet, in a compartment behind Anderson's shirts. The receipt was on the floor of his study." She sat on the bed facing her father. "There's one more thing—I found a huge amount of cash in that secret compartment."

Martin looked at her with raised eyebrows. "And where is the money?"

Nina took a deep breath. "With me. I took everything." She revealed the amount, and he whistled.

"One more reason for Anderson to come after you." He waved the papers. "This is shady business. Something big involving this Dutra guy. Who is he?"

"The CEO of Pharma Innovations."

Martin let out a low whistle and paced the small room. He stopped and looked at Nina. "Did you use any of the money?"

"A little to buy the train ticket and to pay for the first week at the inn. Now I have my own money."

"Don't touch it again."

Nina nodded, heart racing. "What do you think this proves?" *Would Anderson be prosecuted? Would I be considered an accomplice?*

He scanned the papers again. "It might show Anderson is mixed up in a significant operation with Dutra. Pharma Innovations may be involved, which means we're dealing with serious players. It also puts you at greater risk if Anderson suspects you've got this evidence stashed here." He tapped the papers.

Nina's mouth went dry. She licked her lips. "Grace knows a lawyer."

"I think it's wise to get one."

Nina shivered. "I'll call tomorrow and schedule."

Martin sat back down and took his daughter's hands. "I don't want you out of my sight for a single minute. Hear that?"

She widened her eyes and nodded. "That serious, right?" In her desperation to flee home, Nina hadn't considered the repercussion of her act of taking the money and the documents.

Martin nodded. "I'll reach out to my contact on the force. They can take the lead on the case."

Nina recalled the meal paid for by a stranger and the sudden appearance of the jar of horseradish. She could almost feel Anderson's hot breath on her neck, just as he always did when he grabbed her from behind and whispered threats.

CHAPTER 23

Nina squeezed her father's fingers and tried to control the panic that was crawling up her spine like a spider climbing its web. The lawyer, with a sleek, dark bob, took notes on a legal pad on her mahogany desk. The tortoiseshell glasses perched on her nose as she analyzed the details Nina had just given her. In a gray suit, Ms. Reyes put her pen down and looked at Nina from across the desk. Grace had told Nina that a significant portion of Ms. Reyes work involved providing *pro bono* legal services at a woman's shelter. Her advocacy helped marginalized clients who had been silenced by their perpetrators and the legal system, Grace had explained.

With a long sigh, Nina finished detailing what happened in her marriage, guided by Ms. Reyes direct questions. "There's more, but I'm too nervous to go on." She felt her father's fingers pressing hers.

The lawyer gave Nina a reassuring smile. "That's enough for now."

"What are my daughter's options?" Martin, in a checked blazer and dark tie, asked.

"We take emotional abuse seriously. However, it may not lead to criminal charges. You are telling me someone seems to watch you. Keep a detailed record of incidents with dates, times, and description of the incidents. Get witnesses. We can consider a restraining order, but we need evidence. Your situation fits the definition of emotional abuse in this jurisdiction as it includes behavior that causes psychological harm or distress. The manipulation, the isolation, and threats are good examples.

As I said, proving it can be challenging. Fortunately, today there is more awareness of the subject, and we have more legal resources to protect the victim."

"So, I'm not crazy? I mean, this is a crime?" Nina relaxed her shoulders and glanced at her father.

"You're not crazy. Unfortunately, many people live in this condition without realizing they are victims of a crime." Ms. Reyes placed her open hands on the desk. "Since you mentioned a stalker, I suggest always having someone with you. Grace Harbor is safe but ask for help."

Nina unzipped her backpack and pulled out the papers she had brought from home, laying them on the desk. "I found this before I left. This one," she pointed, "lists monetary figures and the name of my husband's best friend. He's the CEO of Pharma Innovations."

Ms. Reyes scanned the document. "I know Pharma Innovations."

"The second is a receipt with a signature I couldn't identify. I also found a large amount of money in a hidden compartment in my closet."

The lawyer examined the papers. "Certainly, there's something strange about this, but for now, we don't have proof that links it to any crime. Keep these papers in a safe place. They could be useful in the future."

At the end of the session, Nina felt as if an anvil had been lifted off her shoulders. It was good to know she wasn't crazy and that there were resources to remove Anderson from her life if worse came to worse. She preferred to leave the topic of divorce for another consultation, despite her father's insistence a few hours before the meeting with Ms. Reyes. The main concern was to make sure she was safe.

Hearing from the lawyer that Anderson's behavior was criminal gave Nina a small dose of courage. The law would be on her side, and she hoped justice would be served. Anderson had stolen her dignity, her sense of identity. He'd wanted to shape her in a way that violated her nature. Throughout the years of marriage, Nina believed she was an inferior being, a worthless woman, an individual without her own will. She heard her so-called friends judging other women who suffered domestic abuse, criticizing them for not leaving their husbands. Nina knew it wasn't easy. Abuse took subtle forms and was cyclical, alternating moments of the spouse's regret with increased violence. Anderson had tried to atone for his crimes, with expensive clothes for Nina, but even that came at a price and generated more abuse.

In moments of greatest crisis, Nina felt as though she were sliding on ice and unable to find her balance. Like every abuse victim, she suffered so much that she felt incapable of making decisions. It had taken Nina six years to gather her courage. Other women endured a lifetime in progressively violent marriages because their circumstances trapped them. Their will to escape drained throughout the years, leaving them powerless.

In Grace Harbor, Nina felt her will returning. She was making plans, even if still uncertain. She wanted to work more at Love at Second Sight and maybe even take a management course to prepare to help Grace in other areas. Nina also wanted to strengthen her relationship with her father after six wasted years. It was good to know that the doctor had taken him off his depression medication. He looked much healthier. Nina wanted him to live long, so they could get to know each other better.

Father and daughter had lunch at Beth's Bistro and recapped what the lawyer had told them. They talked about the good times, when Nina's mother was alive, and life was simpler.

Back at the inn, Nina went to her room, leaving her father in the reading nook. Earlier, Martin had offered to help Esther fix the leaking sink in her cottage. Parker had headed out for the day to manage the family's other inn, Tranquility-by-the-Lake, mentioning he might spend the night there.

Nina opened the desk and took out her journal. She noted everything the lawyer had said and wrote some reflections on the recent events. She had stopped using the word coincidence in reference to her move to Grace Harbor. A supernatural force had guided her there. Everything that happened—missing the train, meeting Grace, becoming friends with Jade, connecting with the girl's family, working at the Little Shop of Broken Hearts, and her relationships—all felt like they had a reason.

She penned a few lines envisioning a day when she could live without Anderson's shadow over her. Free. Free to make her own choices, invest in her career, nurture friendships and embrace all life offered. Nina had so much to live for, to experience and savor.

With renewed energy, she closed the journal and returned it to the drawer. Nina found her father reading a book downstairs.

"Want to take a walk down the boardwalk?" she asked.

Martin returned the book to the shelf. "Sounds great."

"And the leak in the kitchen?"

"Nothing much. It's already fixed. Later, I need to stop by a hardware store. I want to replace some cracked tiles in the kitchen. Esther said it isn't necessary, but I want to help."

"We can do that after the walk."

"I already have the measurements." He grabbed his jacket, which was thrown over one armchair, and put it on.

Nina and her father said goodbye to Esther, who was checking in a family that had just arrived. They stepped out onto the damp sidewalk. At the boardwalk, they bought a bag of chocolate at Silvia's shop after chatting with her. Strolling along the pier, father and daughter chatted about Grace Harbor while savoring their treats. Seagulls swooped and circled above the green waters, where fishermen's lines dipped beneath the surface. The birds appeared to be in a lively discussion, cawing at each other.

"What a charming place, Nina." Martin tossed a small chocolate into his mouth.

Nina swept a hand through her tousled hair, attempting to tame it, as a gust of wind whipped around her. "I think there was a divine conspiracy to bring me here."

Martin nodded. "I have been praying for you all these years. The pain in my heart only eased when I prayed. It was difficult to witness the years slip by with my prayers unanswered."

Nina closed the chocolate bag and tucked it into the pocket of her black hoodie. "I never had the courage to tell you what was happening to me."

"But I knew something was wrong—a father's heart. I may not have known the details, but things were going from bad to worse."

Nina clutched her father's arm, leaning on him as they walked. "Sorry, Dad."

"It's not your fault. Domestic violence generates fear. I dealt with some similar situations at work and saw the panic in people's eyes—women, children, the elderly, even some men—and the excuses victims use for staying where they are."

"Anderson destroyed me."

Martin paused and gently pulled his daughter to the railing, making room for people to pass. "He didn't destroy you. He tried to erase you. But you can find your identity with the support of those who love you. These people love you. Look at Jade and her family. Esther spoke of you with such warmth when I was fixing the tap. And Parker? He's protective of you. I noticed that."

"You've barely arrived!" Nina smiled.

"There are things we only see and understand as we age, like human nature." He kissed her forehead.

They walked toward the open area at the end of the pier, where four fishermen were waiting for their catch. A seagull swooped down in front of Nina and Martin as if trying to scare them away. Nina held onto her father's arm and rested her head on his shoulder, reflecting on what he had just said. Jade and Esther with their care. Parker with his protection.

The breeze brushed against Nina's face, and she sighed. "Dad, do you think I will ever know who I am?"

He squeezed his daughter's hand. "In a way, we all seek to know who we are. Difficult situations blur our perception. I think you're on the right track to discover yourself because you're opening up to new and valuable experiences."

"Do you think God brought me here?"

"Possibly."

"Why did he allow me to suffer?" Nina followed a seagull with her eyes. It would be so wonderful to learn how to fly.

"That's the greatest question of humanity. Why do we suffer? My answer: I don't know. But I'm happy you've found a place to start over."

"I found good friends." Nina closed her eyes and prayed for days without fear.

CHAPTER 24

In the days that followed, Nina experienced a routine that was ideal, the one she had dreamed of. She worked hard, connecting with familiar and unfamiliar faces at Love at Second Sight, learning a bit about the stories behind each broken heart. At the end of the workday, Parker or her father, often joined by Jade, would walk with her to the inn. Supper became a cherished time for them, a time to deepen their bonds.

One evening, Martin arrived just before closing to pick Nina up. She was busy unpacking boxes filled with clothes and decorations while Grace shelved the items. Shirley had come in, an hour earlier, and was immersed in Abel's reading of poetry. His soothing voice echoed through the shop.

"I see you're busy. I'll wait over there." Martin gestured to the reading nook.

"Abel is inspired today." Nina heard the lines of a Shakespearean sonnet.

Martin grabbed a cup of coffee from the kitchenette and joined Abel, Shirley and a couple of other people. Nina opened another box in the storage room, pulling out dresses, shirts and pants. Grace walked in.

"Abel is so excited today." Nina passed several hangers to Grace.

"Wish he could always be like this." Grace hugged the pile of clothes.

Nina followed Grace to the clothing section. Abel had finished reading and started an animated chat with Martin and Shirley, who laughed at something funny he had said. Nina caught snippets of their conversation as she approached the group. The three talked about poetry. It was wonderful to see her father socializing. An extravagant idea struck her—what if he stayed in Grace Harbor permanently? It would be wonderful, especially because she was considering making Grace Harbor her permanent residence. If he did, they could rent a place together. She envisioned herself in one of the charming homes on Main Street or perhaps even by the seaside. What a dream it would be to see Grace and Abel, Shirley, Esther, Jade and Parker every day, and participate more in the community.

"What's got you humming like that?" Grace stopped by Nina's side.

"Was I singing?" Had a song slipped from her lips without her even realizing? It had been ages since Nina had sung. Anderson used to say that her voice was like a shrill when she sang.

"A very cheerful song." Grace smiled.

Nina pressed both hands to her face. "I think I'm happy."

Grace hugged the young woman. "You have no idea how happy I am to hear that. It's the air in Grace Harbor." She winked at Nina and disappeared to the back of the shop.

When Nina finished her work, she approached the lively group. Abel was reciting another sonnet, and her father and Shirley applauded at the end.

"Hi, Nina," Shirley said. "I haven't enjoyed myself this much in a long time."

She smiled. "I see Dad is having a good time, too."

Shirley looked from Nina to Martin. "Oh, he's your father." She introduced herself to him.

"I arrived a few days ago." Martin shook her hand.

Abel laughed. "Love is not love which alters when alteration finds or bends with the remover to remove. Sonnet 116."

Nina found the quote peculiar. In the past, she might have dismissed it as mere coincidence. Not now. She was rediscovering love. Memories surfaced—love is patient, it is not self-seeking. Love always protected, trusted, hoped and persevered. She had learned these Bible verses in Sunday school, but those teachings had faded during her time with Anderson. In

Grace Harbor, she met generous and patient people, just like her parents. As Grace and Parker would say, those blessed much find it in their hearts to give much. Nina anticipated the day she could give much, even though she sensed she was already beginning to share a little of what she had received in this place.

***

Parker missed the family supper because he stayed at Tranquility-by-the-Lake to welcome some last-minute tourists that arrived without a reservation. Esther told Nina and her father that the other inn had a skilled manager, but she was nearing the end of her pregnancy. The person who was supposed to replace her still felt insecure about the job, which forced Parker to spend more time there. Nina had to admit that she missed him at the table. She had already grown accustomed to Parker's calm and pleasant presence and loved to hear his and Jade's banter.

Martin helped Jade with homework that evening, giving Nina and Esther the opportunity to talk while doing the dishes. Exhaustion led everyone to bed soon after ten o'clock. Nina slept peacefully, knowing her father was in the room next door.

Feeling energized, Nina went to work a little earlier the next day. Grace was already in the shop with her husband, who had had a good night's sleep and was more alert. The two women arranged the display window before opening the door.

"I need to leave a bit earlier. Abel has a doctor's appointment." Grace dragged an antique wooden chair and placed it in front of the antique desk in the window.

"That's fine. I need to take inventory after we close." Nina went to the door and unlocked it.

In the afternoon, Martin called to inform his daughter that he was going to the hardware store to buy some tools to repair a few things at the inn.

"Wait for me. I'll pick you up," he said.

"Take your time. I have to take inventory. We've received so many items that we lost track."

Shirley arrived for the poetry reading, and she and Abel took turns reading. Some customers stopped to listen and applauded at the end. Shirley got so excited that she suggested reading plays. Abel gladly accepted, and before closing the shop, they read excerpts from Tennessee Williams' *Cat on a Hot Tin Roof*, much to the delight of Grace, Nina, and the audience.

"You'll soon turn into a community theater," Grace said to the group.

A few hours later, the shop fell silent. Nina locked the door when the last customer left. Her father sent her a brief message saying he would leave the hardware store in a few minutes. Nina responded with a thumbs-up sign.

A noise coming from the storage room sent a shiver down Nina's spine. No one had the key except Grace. Heart racing, she meandered to the room and peeked inside.

"Is anyone there?" Nina's heart raced.

She stepped out of the storage room, her cellphone gripped in her hand. She moved closer to the cash register. Drops of sweat trickled down her back, the dampness absorbed by her gray sweater. She texted her father, finger trembling. The seconds stretched like an eternity. No response from him. A glimmer of hope flickered when she caught sight of pedestrians outside. A middle-aged couple stopped by the shop window and waved at Nina. She waved back, the pressure on her shoulders releasing a bit. Maybe it had been her imagination playing tricks.

She turned when a thud from the storage room echoed through the shop. Her breathing deepened. She ran to the front door and checked if it was locked. Nina looked at her cellphone. Her father was typing something.

LEAVING THE STORE. HEADING YOUR WAY.

Nina dashed to the counter, grabbed her backpack and coat. She returned to the door, glancing back over her shoulder and forward into the street, searching for her father. Another thud echoed from the storage room, and she unlocked the front door, stepping out into the cold air. She turned to lock the door and felt a large hand gripping her arm. Nina screamed and closed her eyes, dropping the key to the floor.

"Nina, it's me."

She opened her eyes and saw Parker's face. She embraced him and rested her head on his chest, her body trembling. "Parker." Her voice came out muffled as she buried her face in his padded jacket.

He wrapped his arms around her, rocking her as if cradling a child. "Shh, shh, I'm here. It's okay, it's okay."

Nina dried her eyes on the soft fabric of his shirt. "There was a noise inside. I don't know what it was."

"Everything's fine." Parker rocked her a little more. Then he pulled her away from his body and looked into her eyes. "I'll go check inside." He bent down to pick up the key from the floor.

"Don't leave me alone." She clutched the sleeve of his coat.

He placed a hand on Nina's shoulder. "Come with me."

Hanging onto Parker's sleeve, she followed him as he turned on all the lights. Together, they moved toward the reading nook, then looked between the clothing racks. Before entering the storage room, Parker asked Nina to wait at the door.

He peered between the boxes. "Is there a back door here?"

Nina nodded and pointed toward some metal shelves. "Back there."

She watched Parker maneuver around the shelves and disappear behind them. Nina heard the door being locked.

Parker reappeared. "The door was unlocked."

Her knees buckled. "Unlocked? I locked it myself when the last delivery arrived this afternoon."

"It's locked now. Strange." Parker moved closer to Nina, wrapping an arm around her shoulders. "Let's get out of here. I'll call the police as soon as we get back home. You need something warm to drink."

Nina let him lead her to the door. "My dad should arrive to pick me up." She checked her cellphone. "He's still two blocks away."

"Tell him to go straight to the inn."

Nina sent the message. Parker took her backpack and locked the front door. Looking from side to side on the street, he pulled Nina close to him with his arm draped around her shoulders.

They stepped into the lit street. Nina leaned into Parker, seeking both the safety and comforting warmth of his body, a rush of relief mingling with great affection.

CHAPTER 25

"The police?" Esther gaped at her brother.

Parker and Nina had just walked into the cottage and summed up what had happened in the shop. "The back door was unlocked." Parker hit a number on his cell phone.

Esther led Nina to the sofa and draped a blanket over her. "You're shaking."

Parker provided the details of the incident to the police, and Nina listened. It all felt strange. She was sure she had locked the door. Living on high alert, Nina took every precaution to avoid an unexpected run-in with whoever was following her. Grace hadn't gone back to the storage room since Nina locked the door. She remembered doing it.

"Grace is going to the shop to talk to the police." Parker sat next to Nina.

"I'm sorry I was late, sweetheart." Martin, in the armchair next to the fireplace, ran his fingers through his graying hair.

"It wasn't your fault, Dad. I just don't understand."

"We need to find out who is stalking Nina. This can't go on like this." Esther raised her hands, exasperated, and went to the kitchen area.

"Who's following Nina?" Jade entered the room, hair wet from a shower.

Nina looked at Parker and made a slight gesture with her hand, showing he should explain the situation to his niece.

He reached out his hand to Jade, pulling her close. The girl sat beside him. "We're not sure."

Jade's eyes widened. "A bad man?"

"Yes, that's possible."

Jade lowered her head and mumbled something.

"What was that?" he asked his niece.

"Does a bad man give gifts?" Her gaze was glued to the floor.

Esther rushed in from the kitchen like an arrow and crouched down in front of her daughter. "What are you talking about?"

The girl squeezed her hands and pressed them to her eyes. "A man gave me a gift. He said it was for Nina."

Esther gasped.

Parker turned to Jade. "What do you mean?"

Jade stood up and ran down the hallway, returning with a flat, square parcel. "The man gave me this. He said it was a gift for Nina."

Martin stood up and grabbed the package, tearing the cream paper, pulling out a blue kite. "What does it mean?"

Jade clung to Parker's arm. "It's a kite. Blue. The man said Nina likes blue."

Nina's eyes darted from one stunned face to the other and stared at the kite. Panic surged through her as she pressed her hands to her forehead, trying to steady herself. The living room spun. "I know Anderson is close."

Jade paused in the middle of the room, tears streaming down her round face. "Is he going to hurt Nina? Did I do something wrong?"

Nina stood up and pulled Jade into an embrace. They sat down. "No, sweetheart, it wasn't you, but this man isn't a good person." Her voice was soothing. Nina didn't want Jade or any of her friends to feel guilt for what happened to her. She stroked Jade's hair, damp with the sweet scent of strawberry shampoo.

"This has gone too far. We're going to the police." Martin pressed his fingers to the bridge of his nose.

Esther sat next to her daughter, who was squeezed between the two women. Parker stood tall, filling the living room with his presence. Nina studied his grim face. He clasped his palms together and rested his face on his fingertips. He paced back and forth. Then he stopped in the middle of the room and shook his arms.

"I'll talk to the sheriff in person tomorrow morning. I also have a friend who is a detective. He can help us gather information about any suspicious individuals in the area." Parker knelt in front of Jade. "Precious pebble, what did the man look like, and where were you?"

"I was leaving school with my friend. I don't know what he looks like. His cap was black, and he was wearing dark glasses."

Esther let out a moan. "Oh, my. What if something had happened to her?"

Nina leapt off the sofa as though she had been pinched. "That's all my fault. Look at what I dragged to Grace Harbor, to you all."

Parker locked his gaze on her. "You didn't bring anything here other than the joy of your presence."

Nina threw her hands up in the air. "Joy? I don't see anyone smiling or celebrating."

"Sweetheart—" Martin walked over to his daughter.

She moved to the corner of the room with her hands pressed against her head. "I carry my unhappiness on my back like a turtle carries its shell. I spread fear like a virus. Anderson will never leave me alone until he has his way. I don't want this for you."

Jade hid her face in her mother's shoulder. Martin sat down again, head lowered.

Parker held Nina by the shoulders, not allowing her to pull away. "No. You don't carry that kind of thing on your back. What we see is a beautiful, caring person. You're hurt, yes, but not an agent of fear. We will get through this together." Parker looked at his sister and Martin. They nodded.

Nina glanced at Jade. "What if something had happened to her? How would I ever forgive myself?"

Jade untangled herself from her mother and hugged Nina. "I'm okay. Look." She stepped back a bit and twirled on her bare feet.

Hot tears streamed down Nina's face. She pulled Jade close and buried the girl's face in her chest. She would do anything to protect Jade. Even if it meant leaving Grace Harbor. She would never allow the horror that had followed her for six years to affect her friends, let alone Jade. The mere thought of Anderson speaking to the girl churned a wave of nausea in Nina's stomach. She fought the urge to scream and run through the streets of Grace Harbor after Anderson like a mad dog ready to attack.

She pulled Jade away from her body. She looked at the faces of the people she loved. "I need to go. I can't allow anything to happen to Jade, can't put you all in a situation you didn't choose to be in. Grace Harbor has become my home. It welcomed me and my broken heart, never judging me, only loving me. But I can't put you at risk." She wiped her eyes with the back of her hands and sniffled.

Martin stood up and hugged his daughter. "I'm here for you."

Esther let out a sob, and Jade rushed to her mother's side. Parker turned to the wall and rested his head against it. Nina clung to her father's arm and looked at Esther holding Jade and Parker with his back turned, his broad shoulders slumped.

Nina let out a long sigh. "I don't know how to thank you for taking me in when I needed it most. The kindness, protection, and love from each of you have found a special place in my heart. Here I found some pieces of my identity. I'll never forget you, not even when everything turns to ashes. She sobbed, tears cascading down her face. "When my life gets back on track, I'll reach out."

Nina wrapped her arms around her father's waist. They walked toward the front door. Her chest burned with the impending separation from those she had learned to love. She would carry with her Jade's sincerity,

Esther's perseverance, and Parker's dignity. From each of them, Nina had learned wonderful lessons. Grace had crossed her path, introducing her to real people facing real struggles. They all shared a common thread—the search to mend their broken hearts.

She glanced at her three friends, her new family, as if taking a mental photograph to remember them forever. Then, she buried her face in her father's shoulder and let him lead her toward the door, the one that would separate her from Jade, Esther, and Parker.

CHAPTER 26

"**N**o!" Parker's deep voice exploded in the room like thunder.

Nina paused with her trembling hand on the doorknob and felt her father's fingers pressing on her shoulders. She stood frozen still like a statue, back turned to Parker, Esther, and Jade. Perhaps it was a delusion, and she hadn't truly heard his tormented voice. She opened the door.

"Nina, don't go." His voice was calmer, but still firm.

It was indeed Parker's voice. Nina turned and was pushed back when Jade lunged at her like a football player and grabbed her around the waist. Nina hugged Jade tightly. The girl was crying and shaking.

Nina glanced at Parker's tense face. His arms dangled at his sides. He stepped closer to her.

"You know I need to do this to protect you all." She wiped her eyes with the sleeve of her hoodie.

"I won't let you live on the run like a criminal. That's not right. It's not fair." Parker walked over to her with his hands clasped as if in prayer.

Nina hugged Jade tighter and looked at Esther, who was crying and nodding her head.

"Don't you understand? Anderson is vengeful."

"Anderson is a coward," Martin said firmly. "He is a manipulative coward. We can't play his game anymore, sweetheart."

Parker walked around the room, scratching his head. "We need a strategy. I'm calling my detective friend right now." He turned to Martin.

"Maybe it's a good idea for you to call some of your contacts and find out what Anderson has been up to."

"Okay." Martin pulled the cellphone from his jeans pocket.

Nina ran her finger along Jade's hair, that was now dry. "What about her? This man was stalking her. This is very serious."

Jade stared at her mother. "I wasn't afraid."

Martin held the girl's shoulder. "I'll walk with her to school and pick her up."

"Good idea," Parker said.

"Thank you." Esther gestured for her daughter to sit beside her. "I'm not always free to walk with her."

"Please, have a seat, Nina." Parker led her to the sofa, pulling her by the hand. "Promise me you won't talk about leaving. Running away is not the solution anymore. It was the best choice when you left home, but now you're safe. Promise that you'll stay."

Nina bit her lower lip and nodded. "I need to be stronger."

Parker crouched beside her. "You are strong. Never doubt that." He took out his phone that was resting on the coffee table and hit some numbers. He walked to the kitchen area and leaned against the counter by the sink.

Martin excused himself, saying he would go to his room to call his police friend, then left.

Esther stood up and sat beside Nina. "You are safe here."

"I feel safe when I'm with you, but the concern you have—I didn't mean to cause all this."

"People only worry when they want what's best for each other. We want the best for you, Nina."

"Uncle Parker likes you, Nina. He told me." Jade pressed her lips with her hands.

Both women turned their heads to Jade. Esther broke the moment of embarrassment, saying,

"We all like Nina."

"I know, but Uncle Parker likes her more. That's why he bought her a present—" Jade covered her mouth again.

Nina stared at Esther, face burning like hot coal.

"What are you talking about, Jade?" her mother asked.

"I can't tell you. He said it was a secret."

Parker entered the living room, all three pairs of eyes on him. "Saul said he and some other officers patrolled the block near the shop. They asked a few people if they'd seen anything strange around. One woman said she saw a man in dark clothing near the shop's back door, but she thought he was a delivery person."

"Was it the same man who gave Jade the kite?" Esther asked.

"I told Saul about it. Hard to tell. Neither Jade nor the woman could describe the man." Parker sat down beside his niece, who hid her head in his chest.

Nina scanned his face. Jade's comment hammered in her mind. Why would he have bought her a gift?

Martin opened the front door and walked in. They all glanced at him. He shoved his hands into his coat pockets. "My police buddy has deployed an undercover officer to watch Anderson's residence. So far, no activity in the last twenty-four hours."

Nina interlaced her fingers. "Anderson is a creature of habit. It's odd that there's nothing going on in or around the house. He leaves for work at seven in the morning and returns at seven in the evening. I've never understood how he's so punctual, being a surgeon. We'd expect shifts and emergency calls from the hospital, but that has never happened."

"My friend is going to hop by the hospital and inquire," Martin said.

"All good then." Parker glanced at the others. "Martin is walking Jade to school and picking her up. We'll gather all the information we can about Anderson and the mysterious bald man stalking Nina and Jade." He walked over to Martin. "If you see anything unusual, please keep me posted."

Esther stood up, visibly fatigued. "I suggest we order pizza. I don't think anyone here feels like cooking."

"Yay!" Jade sprang to her feet as if her worries had vanished.

Nina envied the girl's cheerfulness. The weight on her shoulders was too great, and she felt guilty for bringing concern, and perhaps even danger, to the family. Martin insisted on paying for the food, despite Parker and Esther's protests.

After supper, Esther excused herself and told Jade it was time for bed. The girl didn't complain this time. Her eyes were heavy with sleep. She yawned and followed her mom. Martin put on his coat and said he was going for a walk around the block. Nina knew her father's instincts as a former police officer would never allow him to relax until he was certain she was safe.

Nina and Parker washed the few dishes left in the sink. The steady flow of the tap water and the soft clatter of plates created a soothing rhythm as they worked together. Nina put away the last plate on the shelf while Parker wiped the counter with a cloth.

"Would you like some tea?" he asked.

Nina dried her hands on the dish towel. "I can make us some."

He touched her shoulder and pulled out a chair. "Have a seat. It's been quite a day. I'll make it."

Nina hesitated before complying. She had only experienced being served in the restaurants and parties she went with Anderson. At home, she never deserved to be served, not even a glass of water. She recalled the day she was discharged from the hospital after the appendectomy. Instead of being cared for, she had to cook for Anderson the same day. He insisted she was fit for light household chores, which meant cooking and cleaning the kitchen and the bathrooms. She ended up having a post-surgical infection and returned to the hospital for treatment. Anderson blamed Nina for being careless. She was back the next day with no break from her chores.

She watched Parker turn on the electric kettle and open the cupboard door, pulling a wooden box.

"Which would you like?" He placed the box on the table and opened the glass lid, displaying an assortment of teas.

"Peppermint." She loved herbal tea, despite drinking only black tea back home.

Nina watched as Parker took two mugs from the cupboard and opened the tea packets. A caring man by nature, he had ended two romantic relationships for Jade's sake. He embraced the role of family man even without a wife and children of his own.

Parker set the steaming mug in front of Nina and sat down in the chair beside her, elbows resting on the dining table. He twirled the mug in his hands, sipped some tea, and looked at Nina. "Aren't you going to wear your hair in pigtails anymore?"

She laughed, feeling the tension leaving her entire body. "My hairdresser has been busy with a lot of homework."

Parker smiled. He sipped more tea and settled the mug on the table. "I like your hair."

Nina touched her curls. In her social circle, curls were only accepted when styled artificially. "They seem to have a mind of their own."

"It's a beautiful frame for your face."

Parker, what are you doing to me? The warmth Nina felt rising in her neck wasn't caused by the tea. She lowered her head, concealing a smile.

The sound of the toilet flushing traveled to the kitchen, followed by Jade's muffled complaint. Nina tightened her grip on the mug, and soon felt a gentle touch on her finger.

"Nina, I'm sorry. For what I just said."

She raised her head and looked at him. "Don't apologize. I'm not used to compliments."

"There's so much about you that deserves compliments." He twirled the mug once more.

"Not sure what compliments I'd deserve."

He raised his hand and began to count his fingers. "For one, you're beautiful inside and out. You're respectful and kind. You treat people with sympathy. Everybody around Grace Harbor seems to know and like you."

Nina shrugged. "I work in the most famous shop in town. That's how they know me."

"It's more than that. It's your calm attitude." He lowered his hand and sipped more tea.

She let out a sad laugh. "Calm? I'm so tense that my back feels like an ironing board."

"That's exactly it. Despite what's happening, you're not harsh or bitter. I believe you are tense. The stalking and all, but you remain gracious."

Nina clasped her hands, heart heavy. After a moment, she tapped her chest, her voice trembling. "It hurts, Parker. A lot."

He reached across the table, squeezing her fingers. "I can't imagine how much it hurts. If I had a magic eraser, I'd wipe away all the pain you've endured. No one deserves what you suffered. One day, Nina, I want to see you smile—truly smile, without fear. I want to be the one to bring that joy to you."

Nina swallowed a lump in her throat. Her eyes burned, tears ready to stream down her face. She rubbed her eyes. "You already do, Parker." She offered him a faint smile. "Jade makes me laugh, too. When I'm with you and your family, I forget a bit about my problems. I'm so grateful to you."

He squeezed her fingers again. "I want to be your friend, Nina."

She looked at him, feeling the pressure of his hand and the warmth of his skin. "You already are. You are a great friend." Nina wove two fingers through his.

Their gazes locked, a silent exchange unfolding between them. Nina studied his manly face, searching for hidden messages in the depths of his eyes. Emotions tugged at her heart. Oh, she had so much to share with him! It was comforting and frustrating to feel the touch of his fingers on her wrist. Doubt, hope, sadness, joy. She sensed a connection with Parker that made her heart race.

The only sound in the kitchen was the steady ticking of the clock on the wall. An unexpected warmth spread through her soul. Parker's presence enveloped her in soothing numbness. With a gentle brush of her thumb against his fingers, Nina conveyed a silent message of gratitude. In response, Parker pressed a soft kiss to the tips of her fingers, igniting a heat that flushed her cheeks. Overwhelmed by the sensations, she retracted her hand and placed it in her lap. The tactile memory of his touch lingered, sending tingles through her skin.

Parker lowered his head for a moment. He raised it and sought Nina's eyes. "Nina."

From his lips, her name came out like a brief but profound song.

CHAPTER 27

The dark, yet calm sea before a storm hid many dangers. Nina took Jade by the hand and wrapped her arm around her father's. A week had passed since the mystery of the unlocked door in the shop and the blue kite Jade had received from a stranger. Martin's police friend continued monitoring Anderson's home. Or rather, the lack of activity.

According to him, the doctor had disappeared. No one at the hospital shared information—privacy issues, they said. Nina's fears were not unfounded. A man with such a rigid routine disappearing out of the blue indicated much more than she would like to imagine. Anderson wouldn't get his hands dirty from committing a crime. He would much prefer pulling strings from a distance, hiring someone to torment Nina.

She tugged her father and Jade away from the boardwalk, anxious to go back to the inn and hide in its familiar walls. She was on high alert even with her father by her side.

As they crossed the street toward the inn, Martin guided Nina and Jade in the opposite direction.

Nina looked at her father, frowning. "The inn is that way." She pointed to the left.

"I want to show you something. It's just over there." Martin gestured to a street past a playground.

"A surprise? I love surprises." Jade bounced, yanking Nina's arm.

Martin laughed. "It is a surprise indeed."

Jade let out a shriek as if she were about to receive the greatest gift ever. Nina hoped the surprise wasn't too far away. She followed her father, her right arm bouncing with Jade's jumps.

A block away, they turned onto a narrow, tree-lined street. The houses were small, but charming, mirroring the quaint character of Grace Harbor. A carpet of yellow and red leaves blanketed the sidewalk. Jade kicked a pile of them in excitement at the coming surprise.

"That one." Martin pointed to a powder blue house with white shutters. He opened the gate of the picket fence and invited Nina and Jade to step into the small front yard. "So?"

Nina looked at the house and then at her father. "So, what?"

"The surprise is inside?" Jade stepped onto the porch. "Who lives here?" Her almond-shaped eyes were wide with expectation.

Martin fished a keychain with keys from his pocket and waved them in the air. They jingled as he approached the door. "If all goes well, Nina and I will live here."

Nina felt a mix of anxiety and excitement. "What do you mean?"

Martin inserted the key into the lock and pushed the white door open, signaling for Nina and Jade to enter. Jade rushed in and darted through the living room. The Cape Cod style furniture added warmth to the cozy space. Several paintings lined the walls, depicting boats and coastal scenes.

"Can I see the bedrooms?" Jade dashed down the hallway when Martin nodded.

"What's going on?" Nina walked to the window, looked outside, and then turned to him.

"I decided to move here." He smiled.

Nina rubbed her forehead. "Well, I didn't see this coming."

"Not sure if you're happy or sad?"

She shrugged. "A mix of feelings. You know how attached I've become to Grace Harbor, but this situation with Anderson—"

Martin stepped closer to his daughter. "This situation will be resolved. I have hope."

"So far, we don't know anything. Anderson is missing. He's certainly around or someone else he sent." She let out a sigh.

"We'll catch him soon."

Nina wished she had her father's confidence. She did a spin in the cozy room. It would be a dream to live in a place like Grace Harbor with her father, near Jade, Esther, Parker, and her friends. She even envisioned herself taking on more responsibilities at Love at Second Sight, earning a better salary, supporting herself without having to use Anderson's dirty money.

Jade called for Nina and Martin from the hallway. Nina marveled at the two bedrooms, which followed the same décor style as the living room. The bathroom was spacious and renovated with white tiles and a powder blue vanity. The kitchen had a window above the sink overlooking the backyard, with a crab apple tree shedding its leaves. Nina's heart swelled with a comforting sense of belonging. If she could pick any house in the entire world to call home, she would pick this one. She could see herself making apple pies and inviting Jade, Esther, and Parker over for coffee. She could host a Saturday tea party for Grace and the book club. Abel could recite poems, and the walls of Nina and her dad's home would absorb all the beautiful words created by the immortal writers who lived on through their literature.

In the middle of the kitchen, Nina clasped her hands and brought them to her chest. She looked at her father. "I wish I could say that nothing would make me happier than living here."

"Yay." Jade spun around the table.

Nina wanted to join the girl and spin and spin around the table, clap her hands, and bring her things from the inn to restart her life in this dream house. But her apprehension held her back.

"So, can I close the deal?" Martin placed the keys on the table.

For a moment, Nina thought about saying no. Looking at the kitchen and Jade's joyful face, she agreed.

She held on to the hope that Anderson would be caught, finally allowing her to find peace and a new start in Grace Harbor.

***

"Hold your horses. What? A house? Where?" Parker attempted to rein in his niece, who was bouncing as if on a trampoline.

"I still can't believe it." Nina widened her eyes.

Esther turned around with the coffeepot in hand. "What a fantastic idea!"

Martin took off his jacket and draped it over the back of a chair in the kitchen of the Baek's home. He explained his plan to move to Grace Harbor and the location of the house.

"Oh, I know, that blue one next to Shirley's." Esther began to pour coffee into the cups lined up on the counter.

Nina surveyed her father's expression. Lately, he had been showing up at the shop during Abel's readings, and Shirley was a regular at those literary gatherings. Well, not much of a coincidence, she considered. If her father was getting closer to Shirley, Nina would support him. He had been a widower for quite some time now, and deserved a new start.

"We need to celebrate all this." Parker passed the cups to the adults and filled a glass of orange juice for Jade. "A toast to the new residents of Grace Harbor. May your life here be filled with wonderful surprises."

They raised their cups, voices overlapping with excitement about the news. As Nina sipped her coffee, she studied Parker's face. He wore a smile that suggested he was lost in a special thought. What was that flicker in his eyes? The memory of his lips brushing against her fingers just a week ago lingered, no matter how hard she tried to dismiss it. Nina reminded herself she was still married, and that Parker had only offered her his friendship. Perhaps the glances he gave her expressed appreciation for her consideration toward Jade.

"And when are you moving?" Esther placed her cup in the sink.

"The day after tomorrow," Martin said.

Coffee turned into supper, which Nina insisted on preparing, so that Esther could attend to the guests at the front desk. Jade went to the living room to do her homework and called Martin to help her. Nina considered the prospect of Martin and Shirley becoming a couple. That would be good for both. She chuckled.

"What are you laughing at?" Parker was chopping onions, his eyes filled with tears. He wiped his face with a piece of paper towel and sneezed.

"Nothing much. And why are you crying? Because I'm leaving the inn?" She stirred a sauce in the pot.

Parker let out a laugh and sneezed again. He left the knife on the cutting board and wiped his eyes. "If you ever left Grace Harbor, my tears would be real, not onion-induced." His expression became serious.

Nina felt a flush spread around her neck. Maybe it was the heat coming from the pot. A married woman shouldn't react this way, even if she was married to her enemy. Guilt pricked at her conscience. But Parker stirred all sorts of emotions within her. Good emotions. Great emotions.

He moved closer to Nina. "Sorry, Nina. I didn't mean to make an inappropriate comment." Parker tossed the crumpled paper towel in the trash and washed his hands. He grabbed a towel and dried them. He turned back to her. "I know you're a married woman, and my behavior isn't right." She locked eyes with him and continued to stir the sauce. Parker pressed his forehead with two fingers. "I won't lie that I get upset every time I think about what happened to you. But the truth is, I have great affection for you. Whatever happens, I want to see you happy, and I'd do anything to make this possible."

Nina turned off the burner and set the pot aside. What was Parker saying that made her heart feel so constricted? She covered the pot with the lid and put the spoon in the sink. She took off the apron and hung it over the chair, trying to gather her scattered thoughts as if they were a flock of frightened birds. Meeting his gaze, she said,

"I need to go."

She dashed out, ignoring Parker's calls. She slammed the door behind her and rushed to the inn.

CHAPTER 28

Nina ignored the sixth ping on her cell phone. Lying in bed, she crossed her arms over her eyes. She had teased Parker, and he'd responded in a way she hadn't expected. It was her fault that he made the inappropriate comment. What was she thinking?

Nina raised her left hand and stared at her ring finger with a clear mark from the ring she had worn for six years. Throughout those six years, she had seen it as a shackle. Legally, she was still bound to Anderson, even though he had already broken the agreement to care for and treat her with dignity. She felt like a dog on a long leash, enjoying a false sense of freedom. Soon Anderson would pull the leash.

Warm tears streamed down her face, soaking the pillow. Her feelings for Parker were undeniable, even though she couldn't define them precisely. What she felt for him was different from what she felt for Jade or Esther. It was a warm feeling that surged every time he was around. She also trusted him. Jade's love for him proved he was trustworthy and not a mere façade.

Another ping sounded. Nina stretched her body and grabbed the device from the bedside table. One message was from Esther, calling her to supper. Another was from her father, saying he would eat at Shirley's. The rest of the messages were from Parker, apologizing in various ways, pleading with Nina to let him come to her room to apologize in person.

Going to the bathroom, she washed her face and combed through her messy hair. She took a deep breath and texted Esther that she was coming down.

As expected, Jade chattered the whole time. Esther and Parker remained silent, except for compliments to Nina about the food. Nina caught a few fleeting glances from Parker. She averted his gaze, pretending to be interested in Jade's conversation, which made little sense in her confused mind.

After supper, with the dishes already washed and put away, Esther told her daughter to take a shower, excused herself, and disappeared down the hallway. Parker handed a mug of tea to Nina and invited her to sit in the living room.

Face to face, Nina and Parker sipped their tea in silence, exchanging brief looks. Finally, he set his mug down on the coffee table.

"As I told you in my messages, I want to apologize. I acted like a fool, unaware of my limits. I never meant to hurt you. Seeing your sad face hurt me deeply. I'm sorry."

Nina swallowed a huge lump in her throat. What could she say to this considerate man, with pain etched on his features? She placed her mug on the table and clasped her fingers. "I'm the one who should apologize."

He shook his head. "It's not your fault at all. I should never have behaved so badly."

Nina's heart sank, creating a void in her chest. She wanted to reach out to Parker, feel his warmth again, tell him he was an incredible man and—Nina stopped her thoughts. "Of course I forgive you."

He smiled sadly. "I hope we can still be friends."

Nina's chin trembled. "Always, Parker. Always." With a sigh, she made a move to get up.

Parker raised his hand. "Don't go just yet. Stay a little longer."

Nina relaxed her body. "Is there something else?"

"I just want your company for a little while longer."

"Why, Parker?"

"I want to see with my own eyes that you're okay." He studied her face.

Nina sank into the seat, feeling as if she were diving into a warm bath. She closed her eyes, aware that Parker's eyes were surveying her face. Nina dreamed of days of freedom, days when her deepest desires would be fulfilled. For a moment, she felt floating in the warm water, suspended in a blissful weightlessness, all her problems sinking to the depths of the ocean. With each passing moment by Parker's side, the ache in her chest intensified.

***

Tying the sash of her bathrobe, Nina sat on the bed in her new bedroom and looked at her father. He was seated in the chair next to the desk, with his elbow resting on the white top. Martin had just returned from his date with Shirley. Seeing her red eyes, he had hugged her and asked what had happened. Nina told him about her conversation with Parker in the kitchen but omitted the most intimate details.

"Are you upset with him?" Martin asked.

"No. Parker is a decent man." Nina tugged at an imaginary string from the hem of her robe.

He leaned over, resting his elbows on his knees. "Do you have feelings for him?"

Her eyes widened. "Dad, I'm married."

"That's not what I asked."

Nina sighed. "He's special."

Martin reached out to his daughter, and she took his hand. "Listen, sweetheart. Things are complicated right now, and it's hard to figure out your next steps. I see what's happening between you and Parker."

Nina shook her head. "This is all wrong, being still married, you know." Nina lowered her head and released her father's hand. "But I don't want to go back to Anderson, to that terror."

"You don't need to go back to him. If one thing is very wrong, it is the way he mistreated you."

Nina looked at him. "What do I do now?"

"Anderson broke the vow he made to you. He broke your heart. The abuse you suffered is real. It has left marks in your heart. Anderson didn't care for you, didn't respect you as he should have. Now, he's haunting you. I see the fear in your eyes. How could you go back to him?"

Nina clenched her fists, nails digging into her palms. "Why did I marry him?"

"We do foolish things sometimes. Hard to explain why. But there is forgiveness and hope." Martin stroked his daughter's cheek.

"What should I do now?"

"That is something you need to answer. God will give you direction. In any case, never rush through this process. Allow yourself time to understand what is happening and what the next step is."

"What does God expect from me?" Her voice faltered.

"That you act wisely."

Nina ran her hand across the blue bedspread. "I don't know if I'm wise. Look at this mess I've made because of my foolishness."

"I know you will do what is right now." Martin smiled at her.

"And if I mess up again?"

"That's why there's grace."

CHAPTER 29

Nina opened her heavy eyelids and turned over in the soft bed, tracking the beam of sunlight that filtered through a crack in the white curtain. She stretched her arms and legs as the sound of dishes clinking in the kitchen reached her ears. The rich aroma of coffee soon filled the bedroom, coaxing her out of bed. Her first night in the new home had been peaceful, and it was comforting to know her father was there to protect her.

The cellphone alarm reminded her it was time to get ready for work. Grace had mentioned the day before that they needed to talk. Nina felt a wave of anxiety, thinking she might lose her job, but her friend and boss had assured her that the conversation would be about something Nina would find interesting.

She got out of bed and smoothed the covers. After putting on a new pair of jeans and a tan sweater, both from Love at Second Sight, she followed the direction of the coffee aroma. She kissed her father and sat down at the table. "Are you going to make me breakfast every day?" She grabbed a fresh bun from a tray sitting on the round table.

Martin set the coffeepot on the table and sat down. "Can I pamper my daughter?"

"Any time." Nina smiled and spread butter on the soft bun.

"Did you sleep well?" He poured two mugs of coffee.

"Very much. Too bad I can't enjoy the bed longer."

Nina and her father had moved in the day before. With the house being furnished, they only needed to buy food and essential items. Nina had left the inn with a heavy heart. She would be a few blocks away from Jade, Esther, and Parker, but it felt like miles away. The awkwardness between her and Parker didn't last long. Nina admired his spontaneous, yet thoughtful way. He kept a certain distance from her, but remained attentive. Nina was determined to follow her father's advice to take each step at the right time.

"Shirley invited us over to supper tomorrow." Martin sipped his coffee.

"Another date?" She smiled.

He nodded. "She's warm and kind."

"So, things are getting serious between you." Nina nibbled on the bun, the salted butter melting in her mouth.

"We want to get to know each other better. We're more than happy to spend time together. Let the relationship grow."

"That's good, Dad."

They finished breakfast and walked to the shop together. Afterwards, Martin would stop by the inn to take Jade to school. Nina had promised the girl that she would bring her over for supper at her new home that evening.

"I'll pick you up after work." Martin kissed his daughter and left for the inn.

Nina opened the shop and started arranging the new merchandise in its designated spots. Grace soon arrived, accompanied by Abel, his expression hollow.

"One of those days?" Nina hung some shirts on the rack while studying Grace's tired face.

"It's exhausting." Grace had a swollen face and heavy eyes.

"I wish I could help you more."

"That's what I want to talk to you about. First, I'm making coffee for Abel and settling him with a good book."

"Let me." Nina hurried to the corner and turned on the coffeemaker, preparing a mug for Abel.

Grace took him to the couch and picked a poetry book from the shelf, handing it to him.

"Here you go." Nina offered the mug to Abel.

Abel was looking out the window while holding the book and the mug.

The conversation between the two women didn't happen until after lunch, as it seemed everyone had gone shopping that morning. When things quieted down, Nina and Grace leaned against the counter. Abel was more alert and was reading some poems to an older couple.

"What did you want to tell me?" Nina's anticipation urged Grace to get to the point before another customer came in.

"It's about the shop. I've been exhausted and need a break to rest." She rubbed her chubby hand over her eyes.

"And how can I help?" Nina considered working more hours to do Grace's job.

"Being my partner."

Nina's eyes widened. "Partner? I don't have money to invest." She thought of Anderson's money. Her father had said Nina would know how to fix her mess by being wise. She was determined to make choices rooted in integrity, using her own effort and hard work to make her dreams a reality. She wanted to build her future on a foundation of honesty and self-respect.

Grace waved her hand in the air. "I don't want money. What I need is your help. Everything is paid for. Those blessed much find it in their hearts to give much."

Nina smiled at the much-repeated motto. "It might seem like I'm taking advantage of you."

"Are you?" Grace raised an eyebrow and smiled.

"Never."

"I have no doubt about it. I spoke with Ms. Reyes, the lawyer. She can draft a contract. If you ever consider buying me out and taking full ownership of the shop, just let me know. We can work out a plan."

Nina looked at the shop with fresh eyes. The affection she had for that place swelled in her chest like a big party balloon. It was at the Little Shop of Broken Hearts that she had met wonderful people, with their sorrows and struggles, but determined to move forward. Some issues would remain, like Abel's degenerative illness. Nina had to come to terms with the realization that her problem with Anderson would never be resolved. The choice before her was clear: Would she let him shatter the goodness in her life or would she stand firm in what she could control? With a loving father, supportive friends, a job and a beautiful home, Nina had every reason to hope. And God was with her.

"Yes. I want to make plans, Grace." She smiled.

"What a divine encounter it was at the train station." She clasped the young woman's hands and thanked her.

The bell dinged, and Grace greeted the customer, an older woman Nina knew had Parkinson's. Soon they were catching up on the latest news about the town.

"My shop." Nina meandered through the shop, whispering the words to herself.

CHAPTER 30

After phoning the lawyer and scheduling a meeting to discuss the partnership, Grace bid Nina and Jade goodbye and left the shop. She opened the umbrella before closing the front door behind her. With the memory of the open back door a few days ago still haunting her, Nina double checked the locks of both doors. Relieved, she returned to the counter and started reconciling the cash with the receipts. Nina had learned so much from Grace since being hired. Thinking that she would soon be a partner at the shop made her heart jump with excitement.

The rain lashed against the storefront, thick drops splattering off the window. Jade was curled up in an armchair reading a book. Occasionally, she would glance at Nina, seeking reassurance whenever a thunder rumbled outside. Martin had dropped the girl off at the shop after school and rushed to the hardware store. A pipe had burst in one of the rooms of the inn, and Esther needed his help to get it fixed. Parker was due to arrive from Tranquility-by-the-Lake, but the heavy rain had delayed his plan to meet Nina at the end of her workday.

"Nina, I don't like thunder. They scare me." Jade covered her ears with her hands as another clap of thunder echoed through the shop.

Nina closed the cash drawer and walked over to the girl. "Thunder is just a loud noise. It won't hurt you. We'll go home as soon as my dad returns from the store."

The girl's face showed concern. "What if the windows break? I can feel the room shake."

"I don't think they'll break." Nina patted on her shoulder.

"But I saw a video of a hurricane. It broke windows and trees. Where do people hide when there's danger?" She closed her book, eyes wide.

A flash of lighting ripped through the dark sky, illuminating the shop. The girl frowned, trying to be brave.

"Well, people hide in the basement, closets or under the staircase. But don't worry. This isn't a hurricane."

Jade looked around and nodded. She opened the book after the thunder subsided. Nina returned to the counter and worked for a while, keeping an eye on Jade.

The excitement about being a partner in the shop returned. Nina couldn't wait to share some ideas she had with Grace. The reading nook had so much potential for attracting customers. She wondered if Shirley would help. Nina chuckled. The silver-hair woman and Martin were spending more and more time together. No wonder he had also considered starting his own home improvement business. Things were falling into place for both. They were taking root in Grace Harbor.

Nina locked the cash register and headed to the storage room after telling Jade to stay put. A book about animals had finally distracted the girl.

In the storage room, Nina opened one box and surveyed its content. Tomorrow she would price the items and display them in the storefront. Among knick-knacks and cookware, there was an old candlestick, its surface worn with age. Nina lifted and examined it. A little polish would bring it back to life.

The rain still hammered against the roof. An unusual sound caught Nina's attention. Peering through the storage room door, she saw Jade still lost in her book. Dashing to the front door, she checked the lock one more time. Safely locked.

Jade looked at her over the book and smiled. Maybe Nina's imagination was playing another trick on her. As she returned to the storage room, a sudden draft brushed against her face, sending her heart racing. The back door was ajar, swaying in the wind. A wave of dizziness washed over her, her heart pounding in her ears. She grasped the shelf for support, her pulse quickening. She shut her eyes when she sensed a breath, hot and thick, on her neck.

"Catarina, we finally meet again."

Her knees buckled as she felt Anderson's fingers brushing through her hair. A shiver raced up and down her spine and limbs, fear gripping her heart. She wanted to scream at the top of her lungs, but this would send Jade out of the shop into the storm. Panic clawed at her throat as she weighed her options, desperate to protect her vulnerable friend.

Mustering some courage, Nina turned to him. She clenched her teeth, her bottled anger spewing like steam from a boiling kettle. "Get out of here, out of my life."

He flashed a creepy half-smile. "I came to take back what is mine."

She clenched her fists. "I am not yours."

"That's not what our marriage certificate says."

"You hate me." Disbelief crashed over her. How could she ever have loved him, ever trusted him? His face looked distorted in the yellow light of the room.

"We can make things right." He used his velvety tone.

"You can never fix this. It's over." She gritted her teeth.

Anderson ran his hand through her hair with a smirk. "Life seems tough here. Look at your hair. No salons around?"

Nina's blood boiled, and her mind cleared. How had she given herself to that man? "Life here is better than ever."

"You found a boyfriend. Very nice, Catarina. How does adultery feel?"

"I have friends, something you'll never have. Real friends." Nina had been blind, but saw clearly now. Anderson was a sad, pathetic man. He seemed smaller, weaker.

"A silly girl in flashy clothes." The half-smile returned to his face.

Jade's concerned voice called out for Nina.

"Sweety, stay where you are. I'm coming." She stared at Anderson, her temples pulsing.

The girl's voice grew louder. "But who are you talking to?"

"Stay where you are, Jade. Now."

"Your silly friend doesn't understand what you're saying." Anderson laughed.

Nina slapped his face, pleasure replacing fear. She darted past him toward the door, but he grabbed her by the hair, pain flashing through her head.

"If you try something foolish, I won't spare your friend." He pulled out a syringe from his coat pocket. "I'll fix you, and everything will be fine." He raised the syringe and aimed it at Nina's neck.

She squirmed. Anderson twisted her arm, and she let out a muffled scream. Where was Jade? Her vision blurred. The floor seemed to shift under her feet. She started falling, Anderson's arm holding her by the neck. She coughed.

Anderson shouted and his arm flopped to the side, releasing Nina. She stumbled, but quickly regained her balance.

At the doorway, Jade screamed while swinging the candlestick in the air. Anderson fell to the ground, blood dripping from his forehead.

"You stupid girl." He let out a groan.

Jade ran back to the sales floor, crying. Nina skipped over Anderson, but he grabbed her ankle. Twisting her body, she broke free and rushed to the reading nook, desperately looking for Jade. A cold draft surged into the shop. The front door stood ajar, the bell jingling.

"Jade," Nina yelled as she dashed to the door. Lightening stroke and illuminated the deserted streets. Jade couldn't have left and disappeared in such a short time. Nina turned back inside the shop, pushing aside hangers, furniture, and boxes. "Sweety, where are you?"

Anderson emerged from the storage room, let out a roar of rage and rushed toward Nina. She ran out the door, the icy rain slashing against her face. She sprinted down the sidewalk, shouting for help. Her wet hair clung to her face, and her soaked feet splashed through the puddles. Strong hands grabbed her from behind, and Nina thought it was the end. She kicked out in the air, trying to break free.

The deep voice whispered in her ear, "It's me, Parker."

Nina crumpled in his arms, tears and rain mingling on her cheeks. She told him what had happened in the shop. "I think Jade ran away."

A lightning bolt split the dark sky. Parker held Nina at the waist. "My car is right there. Let's look for her. I'll call the police."

Soaked, they climbed into the car. Within seconds, Parker called the police, giving a precise report of the situation and informing them that Jade was missing.

"Let's go back to the inn. Maybe Jade ran back home." He started the car, rain pelting against the windshield.

Nina's teeth rattled from the cold and concern. "I was supposed to take care of Jade and failed."

Parker's eyes met hers. "You were attacked. It's not your fault." He brushed his wet hair from his face.

When they arrived at the inn, Esther was in the reception area, pacing back and forth. She rushed to Nina and Parker, eyes wide with concern. "What happened? Why are you soaked? And where is Jade? I've had a bad feeling all day."

Nina felt guilt swept over her. She began to speak, but her voice faltered. Parker took his sister by the shoulders and summarized the situation. "We've already notified the police."

Esther rubbed her forehead and started pacing again. "Jade will be fine. She's stronger than we think." She spoke as if to convince herself.

Seeing the worry etched on Esther's face, Nina's heart raced with the urge to run into the street to search for Jade. A knot twisted in her stomach as Esther buried her face in her hands, letting out a heart-wrenching sob that echoed in Nina's ears.

Nina clenched her hands and then tossed her hair back. "I'm going out to look for Jade." She sprinted toward the door, but Parker grabbed her arm.

"That's the job of the police. And we don't know where Anderson is," he said.

Martin entered the inn, drenched from head to toe. "I heard what happened. I stopped by the shop, and the police were there."

"What if Anderson took Jade?" Nina shouted.

Esther wrapped her arms tightly around her brother. Martin dropped the shopping bag to the floor and pulled his daughter close. Fear coursed through Nina's body like a thousand lightning strikes.

If anything happened to Jade, she would never forgive herself.

CHAPTER 31

Martin released Nina from his arms. She surveyed the anxious faces mustered in the inn's reception area. Their concern was palpable. And it was her fault. "I have to do something, help the police."

Martin put his hand up. "Don't. I'll go."

Esther grabbed the older man by the arm. "Please, find my Jade."

He nodded and stepped out into the dark street. Nina ran to the door and saw his shadowy figure turn the corner. Turning back, she caught sight of Esther, tears streaming down her face as she leaned against Parker. Nina made a choice.

She dashed outside, raindrops splattering against her face. Parker's voice called after her. She pressed on, lungs burning, unsure where to go.

The boardwalk.

Jade liked the candy shop. If she hadn't gone back to the inn, it made sense for the girl to seek shelter in one of her favorite places that kept its doors open late. Nina sprinted down the street, her feet splashing rainwater accumulated on the sidewalk. A flash of lightning illuminated the boardwalk and the pier in the distance. The lights of the seaside shop flickered in the rain. Nina called out Jade's name until her throat hurt, but only the thunder answered.

As she approached the candy shop, her heart nearly stopped. A red neon sign announced: Closed. Nina ran along the sidewalk. All the shops were shut. She ran back and forth, calling for Jade. Hopeless, she made her way toward Main Street.

What felt like an eternity later, a patrol car rolled up, lights flashing as it pulled over. Nina stopped, hands on her chest. An officer stepped out of the passenger side.

"Catarina Adams?"

Nina blinked, the raindrops blurring her vision. "Yes."

"I need you to come with us." The lanky officer opened the back door of the cruiser.

"You found Jade?" She attempted a smile, but the officer's expression showed no signs of good news.

The officer took off his cap and wiped his face with the sleeve of his dark shirt. "Do you know Anderson Phillips?"

They finally got him. I'm free! "Yes. He's my husband."

"You need to come with us to the station for a statement. He was found dead in a hotel room." The officer spoke in a steady tone as if accustomed to delivering bad news.

**

Nina stepped into the police station, sandwiched between two officers. A female officer with olive skin was waiting for her. Nina's knees threatened to buckle. She felt like a protagonist in a thriller. Jade was missing, her husband was dead, and her father was somewhere searching for the girl. Parker and Esther were probably boiling with anger at her. In an instant, the fragile sense of order she had been clinging to crumbled beneath the weight of the storm. Everything around her seemed to dissolve in the downpour. Her world in Grace Harbor was also collapsing, like every other sandcastles she built. Everything she touched was destined for ruin.

Nina trailed behind the female officer, who pointed to a door in the narrow corridor with gray walls. The fluorescent lights flickered overhead, casting a sad glow to the sterile atmosphere of the precinct. The sound of distant voices and the clatter of keyboards filled the air, mingling with the occasional ringing of phones.

"Follow me." The uniformed woman opened the door to a room with a table and three chairs. "Sit down."

Nina took a seat, her teeth chattering from the chill and fear. Was she considered a suspect in Anderson's death? She had alibis except for the time spent roaming the streets looking for Jade. How much time had elapsed? An hour? Two?

Another officer, older and tired, joined the female officer in the interrogation room. Nina recoiled in her seat when they closed the door.

"You have the right to a lawyer," the tired looking officer said.

A lawyer? I didn't do anything. "I don't understand."

"Your husband was found dead in his hotel room. We don't have any suspects at this point, and the only individuals who knew him are you and your father." The officer leaned back in his chair and studied Nina.

As the words sunk in, her mind raced, then went blank, unable to process what was happening. Her gaze darted to the female officer, but she didn't take her eyes off the yellow pad. Nina was alone.

"Where's my father?" she asked, her voice barely a whisper.

"On his way," the male officer said.

The door swung open, and Martin stepped inside, followed by Leticia Reyes, the lawyer. Relief washed over Nina as she rushed to him, collapsing against his shoulders. Then she pulled back.

"Have you found Jade?" Fear clawed at her chest.

Martin ran his hand on his daughter face. "Parker found her in the shop. She said you told her not to leave. She was hiding inside a wardrobe with linen." He smiled.

Nina laughed and cried with a mix of relief and joy. "Jade, my sweet Jade." She longed to pull the girl into a tight embrace to celebrate her bravery.

"Parker is out there. I've never seen a man in such distress," Martin said.

The female officer left and returned with a gray blanket, giving it to Nina. She draped it around her shoulder.

"He hates me. He and Esther." Nina tightened the blanket around her body.

"No. They are worried about you. Parker is worried sick. They don't blame you. In fact, they praise your courage when Jade told them you fought with the bad man when he pulled you by the hair."

The officer cleared her throat, drawing their attention to Ms. Reyes. The lawyer's voice was firm when she demanded to know why her client was being detained.

"Ms. Adams had no alibi that would account for the time she roamed the streets," the older officer said.

Ms. Reys approached the table and crossed her arms. "We know Ms. Adams couldn't possibly walk all the way to the hotel where her husband was found dead."

Another officer entered the room with a folder. The female officer opened it, read a few things and passed it on to the older officer, who stood up. He scratched his head as he read it. He looked up at Nina.

"Were you aware that your husband used drugs?" he asked.

Drugs? Would Anderson jeopardize his career over an addiction? Yet, the fragments of conversations Nina had overheard hinted at something shady—the names and figures on the paper, the cash.

All eyes were on her when she answered,

"I didn't know."

"Where are the papers you showed me the last time we met?" Mr. Reyes asked.

"In my room." Nina tightened the blanket around her shoulders.

Martin crossed the room to the door. "I can get them."

In less than fifteen minutes, he returned with the document in a plastic bag and handed it to the officer, who said,

"Interesting. We'll use it as evidence."

"If there are no additional questions, my client will go home," Ms. Reyes said to the officers.

"Yes, of course." The older officer studied the document.

Martin took his daughter by the arm and headed toward the door. At the lobby, Nina's gaze found Parker, who was pacing anxiously. He turned to her, and their eyes locked. Parker closed the distance between them, wrapping his arms around her. The blanket slipped from Nina's hands and fell to the floor as she clung to his neck, tears streaming down her face as she sobbed her apologies.

"That was not your fault. You were both brave," he whispered in her ear. "I'm taking you home now."

Home. What a sweet sound. She wanted to run to the comfort of her new home, take a shower, and wrap herself in the soft robe. She wouldn't let remorse or guilt plague her anymore. Yes, it was sad that Anderson's brilliant career had ended in tragedy. Nina felt sorry for him because he would never experience happiness.

For six long and painful years, Anderson had defined who she was. It had been a time of darkness and deceit. Catarina Phillips, shaped in his image, was also dead. Nina Adams was emerging, with a new sense of purpose. In Grace Harbor, she had found the freedom to grow into the person she was meant to be, the image God had intended for her.

Maybe in a few days, the reality of Anderson's brutal death would sink in and bring her sorrow. She would deal with it later. For now, she was relieved Jade was safe. Relieved she could work, go for walks alone and make friends without Anderson's threats. Nina never understood why the man had always been so bitter and vindictive, and it was too late to ask this question.

What she wanted now was home.

CHAPTER 32

Nina slipped into the soft robe and ran a towel through her wet hair, the scent of honeysuckle lingering in the remaining steam of the shower. Parker's voice echoed in the hallway, blending with her father's as it drifted into her bedroom. They would have a long night ahead, hoping for more answers about Anderson's death.

The weight of the tragedy had begun to sink into her heart. Although she had always desired a life away from Anderson's abuse, murder had never been in her thoughts. Breathing in, Nina combed her hair as she looked around. Oh, how she felt at home in the cozy little house her father had rented! Her bedroom was the size of her closet in Anderson's house (funny that she never thought of it as her home). Yet, the wall and the coastal-style furniture seemed to hug her.

Leaving the comb on the dresser, Nina headed to the kitchen. Parker and her dad, each holding a mug of steaming coffee, looked up as she entered. Martin stood up to pour coffee for his daughter as Parker motioned for her to sit next to him. He wore a dry shirt that Nina recognized as her father's, though his hair was still damp.

Parker squeezed Nina's hand. "I called Esther, and Jade is already asleep. They'll drop by tomorrow morning. They want to see you and make sure you're okay."

"What a mess." She curled her fingers around the mug, its warmth comforting against her palms. A sense of calm eased the weight of her worries. Having Parker and her father in control of the situation felt good.

Martin sat down. "It's over."

It seemed like a cruel comment. Yet, memories of the past six years raced through Nina's mind. What could drive someone so talented to be so vindictive and greedy? "It's an unfortunate ending."

Martin walked over to his daughter and massaged her shoulders. "From what we heard, Anderson was implicated in the illegal distribution of opioids. And he didn't work alone, of course. His death was probably some kind of retribution. Ms. Reys is gathering more information."

Nina rotated the cup in her hands, apprehension tightening her stomach. "Do you think I'll be implicated?"

Martin sat down and squeezed Nina's hands. "You have nothing to hide. The police and Ms. Reys will make sure the investigation focuses on the real suspects."

"What about the house?" Her gaze traveled between her dad and Parker.

"That's a separate issue. Ms. Reyes will explore the options," Martin replied.

"And the money?" She asked.

"Again, the lawyer will figure these things out." Martin stood up. "I'm calling Shirley. We spoke earlier, and she was very concerned." He kissed the top of his daughter's head, thanked Parker for his support, and went to his bedroom.

Nina twisted a loose strand of wet hair. "I never thought I'd be the center of such chaos."

"Anderson was the center of it all. You were his target, not the cause of anything." Parker leaned closer, studying Nina's face with intensity.

"Anderson made me believe everything that went wrong was my fault. Will I ever heal from this?"

Parker brushed his fingers against hers. "No matter how long it takes, I'll be here for you. Always."

Nina offered him a shy smile. "I hope so."

"You can count on it." He smiled.

In the days that followed, the investigations progressed, and Nina's connection with the Baek family deepened. Esther reassured Nina of her gratitude for the friendship she shared with Jade and the rest of the family. Nina felt joy as Jade repeated the same story to everyone she knew, that Nina had protected her against the mean man.

The sun returned, along with trips to the beach to fly kites. They no longer had to stay on guard. Nina could enjoy her freedom at last.

Grace had been horrified at the danger Nina had faced in the shop and had a locksmith install electronic locks with alarms, even though she knew Anderson was no longer a threat. The police already had a suspect, and they believed it was the man sent to follow Nina.

A month passed, and the autopsy revealed Anderson had had high doses of a lethal drug in his system. The syringe had his fingerprints and those of another person. Martin told his daughter that the police had contacted Soros Dutra, one of the suspects. According to Ms. Reyes, the director of the pharmaceutical company had had questionable business dealings with Anderson.

The stalker targeting Nina was caught trying to break into Anderson's house, looking for some documents and money. The police said he had previously been employed by Anderson and Dutra, doing illegal jobs. Because he had been in Grace Harbor in the days before Anderson's murder, he became the primary suspect in the case.

The authorities released Anderson's body, and Nina arranged for his burial at the cemetery in the nearby town. The only family he had was his mother, who suffered from dementia and lived in a nursing home in Cleveland. Anderson had had little to no contact with her. So, Nina, Martin and Parker gathered for the solemn occasion as the casket was lowered into the grave.

The following week, Grace and Nina signed the partnership contract at Ms. Reyes' office. The money left by Anderson, along with some assets, would be transferred to Nina. Ms. Reyes was managing the estate, or at least what was left of it since Anderson had debts. The money Nina had found in the closet had never been claimed, so she donated it to a charity that supported children with special needs.

Shirley took over The Little Shop of Broken Heart's book club, attracting more people from neighboring towns. Abel participated but became increasingly distracted. Grace spent more and more time taking care of her husband, with the support of her friends.

The week's big surprise was the announcement of Martin and Shirley's engagement. They celebrated it with family and friends at a beach picnic. Her son, Jonathan, and his wife promised to come over to visit as soon as their newborn baby would be old enough to be on a plane.

The couple set up tents, and Parker lit a bonfire. Despite the chilly winter evening, the guests, wrapped in blankets, enjoyed steaming hot chocolate and spiced cider. Nina moved through the crowd, her royal blue jacket standing out against the darker tones of the season. She served up treats provided by Beth, greeting each guest.

Jade enjoyed the last rays of sunshine, flying kites with Parker. Grace settled Abel in a beach chair with a blanket and a book. Esther tended to the food table while Shirley introduced her fiancé to those who had not yet met him.

Nina gazed at the familiar faces around the bonfire, her heart swelling with gratitude. Just a few months ago, she had fled to an uncertain future, unsure of where she would land. Now, here she was, enveloped by warmth and laughter.

She had arrived home.

The word coincidence felt like an obsolete term, replaced by blessing.

"Nina, come!" Jade handed her the kite. "Your turn." The girl ran to her mother's side, who held out a plate of food for her.

Parker glanced at Nina. The fading light of the setting sun bathed his features. The breeze tousled his thick, dark hair as he pulled the kite and set it down on the sand. "Want to take a walk?"

"I do." Nina's fear had long melted away.

They strolled through the streets of Grace Harbor, leaving the lively celebration behind, the sounds fading into the distance. They reached the pier as the last light of day slipped beneath the horizon. The salty wind played with her curly hair as she accepted Parker's arm.

At the end of the pier, a solitary fisherman packed his gear and headed off, leaving the couple leaning against the safety railing.

"It feels wonderful living without fear." She tucked a strand of hair behind her ear.

Parker turned to her. The dim light from a lamppost illuminated his face. "I've always prayed God would take away your fear. At times, I also prayed for us, here, together. I'm so sorry all this had to happen."

Nina's heart rate quickened. "Anderson paved a dangerous path for himself."

"I want your path to be safe and beautiful from now on." With a tender smile, he reached out and tucked another strand of hair behind Nina's ear.

"I found my safe place."

"I hope to enjoy this freedom with you."

Nina cupped Parker's face with both hands. "And that is my greatest wish."

Parker traced his fingers over Nina's eyes, lingering on her nose and ears before finally brushing against her lips. With a gentle pull, he drew her closer until their mouths met. Nina sighed softly, her heart racing as she rose onto her tiptoes and wrapped her arms around his neck, savoring the sweetness of the moment as they melted into each other.

The pier seemed to float away from its columns. Nina surrendered to Parker's kiss, which was both tender and fervent.

"I'm crazy about you. I love you," he whispered. His lips found hers again with urgency, sending shivers through her body.

Nina's response came moments later once her lips were free. "I love you, too," she said, her heart racing. How wonderful it felt to say these freeing words!

There was no fear in love. Love had transformed her life, not only through Parker, but also Jade, Grace, Esther and her father. Above all, through God's enduring love for her. Nina whispered a silent prayer of gratitude, with her head resting on Parker's broad shoulder.

Parker kissed Nina's cheek and, with a half smile, he fished something from the pocket of his jacket. He opened his hand and showed a little black velvet bag. "I bought this some time ago, not sure when to give it to you. Hope you like it."

Eyes sparkling, Nina took the present and opened it, thinking of the time Jade had almost revealed her uncle's secret about buying something for Nina. She peeked inside and pulled two glass figurines from the bag. Nestled in the palm of her hand, a turtle and an octopus glowed in the light of the lamp post. Nina blinked away the tears and closed her hand, protecting the little creatures. With her heart full of love, she looked at Parker. "How did you know?"

He covered her hand with his. "I saw your collection on the dresser. Thought you might like to add more pieces."

Nina put the figures back in the bag and hugged Parker. She told him about the collection of fine crystal pieces she had been forced to return.

He cupped her face with his hands. "Whatever makes you happy is important to me."

Nina threw her head back and laughed with delight. "I love you even more, Parker Baek."

When they returned arm in arm to the party, their close friends turned to the couple with knowing smiles. Some raised their glasses as if celebrating the news. Her father, hand in hand with Shirley, winked at her in silent approval.

Grace walked over to Nina, eyes sparkling with delight. She planted a kiss on the young woman's cheek.

"Oh, you two! Miracles are never mere coincidences."

"You are absolutely right." Nina beamed with happiness.

Jade, who was resting beside her mother in a chair, sprang up as she saw Nina and Parker. She dashed over to them, eyes wide. "Are you two dating?"

Nina bit her lip and waited for Parker to respond.

"My precious pebble, how would you like Nina to become part of our family for real?"

Nina met Parker's gaze as he turned to her with a smile. Just then, someone switched off the music. The soothing sound of the waves filled the air. Jade leaped into the center of the gathering, spinning with her arms outstretched.

"Nina is going to be part of my family, hehe, hehe, hehe."

Laughter erupted among the guests. Parker took Nina's hands in his, and leaned in close to whisper in her ear,

"That's what I want. Would you like to be my family? For real?"

She ran her fingers through his hair and pulled him closer. "I do, Parker. I do."

The beach party continued late into the night. No one cared about the cold wind on that memorable starlit night.

Nina's broken heart was being mended with the glue of love. With the glue of Parker's love.

In Grace Harbor, Nina discovered the power of grace. Catarina had felt undeserving of happiness because her identity was distorted. Nina was now being transformed into the person God intended her to be. Those blessed much found it in their hearts to give much.

Nina had much to give.

CHAPTER 33

The foundation would be built on solid ground. Nina's sandcastle had collapsed a year earlier. God's grace had reached her through a divine encounter with Grace at a train station. Nina had been lost. Now she was found. That was the kind of grace she and Parker enjoyed together.

The vintage blue dress with a flared skirt hung on the closet door. Sitting on the bed with rumpled sheets, Nina smiled. She wanted to feel beautiful for her husband, who lay snoring softly under the white and blue bedspread in their honeymoon suite.

Far from everything, the cottage stood on the edge of a rugged coastline. Nina inhaled the smell of aged wood and the hint of smoke from the fireplace. She peeked through the curtains. The golden light of the rising sun made the seawater glisten as the gentle waves lapped against the rock.

The cottage on a rock. A perfect illustration of what she and Parker had promised before friends, family, and God at their simple, yet meaningful wedding ceremony. The couple had exchanged their vows in the gazebo at Tranquility-by-the-Sea. Jade had carried the rings, smiling with delight as she declared that Nina was officially her new aunt. Grace Harbor witnessed to the union of two souls who had faced struggles and heartbreak, but had discovered the path to healing together.

Nina and Parker committed to building their home on the solid rock of God's grace and love.

Nina felt a tug on her blue silk nightgown and threw herself back, falling into Parker's bare arms. Her heart was embraced when he held her close.

"Your side of the bed felt empty," he whispered in Nina's ear, leaving a kiss on her neck.

"I'm right here, and not planning to leave." She playfully bit his muscular arm.

Parker pulled Nina down under the covers and ran his fingers through her hair. "All because of the pigtails."

Nina lifted her face and kissed his lips. "How so?"

"When I fell in love with you. Your pigtails." He tucked his hand under Nina's hair.

"Oh, and the blue eyeshadow." She laughed.

"The makeup was a bit much, but the hair—"

"I don't think I should go around with pigtails."

"No. The hairstyle is just for me."

Nina studied Parker's features with loving eyes and fingers. She glanced back at the blue dress she had worn the night before for a cozy supper with her husband right there in the cottage. He had cooked for her. Nina felt like the most pampered woman in the world. And the crazy thing was that she loved it because his efforts came from love. That made it even more special.

"What else do we have planned for today besides strolling along the beach, hand in hand?" He propped himself up on his elbow, his face close to Nina's.

Nina pushed him to lie back down. She snuggled into his embrace and rested her head on his chest. "First, I want to kiss you until I run out of breath."

Parker pulled Nina closer. "I like that. Keep going."

She ran her hand across his face. *My husband.* "Then, fly a kite. What else?" She laughed.

He burst out laughing. "You keep surprising me, Nina."

The two remained in the embrace for a while, listening to the music of the sea. Then, Nina squeezed Parker's hand. "Why do we have to go through so much pain before we find happiness?"

"It's a question I dare not answer. What I know is that, when we least expect it, we have an encounter with grace."

Nina ran her fingers under her eyes, drying a few tears. Parker propped himself back up on his elbow and looked at his wife.

"I made you cry." He brushed off the tears from her eyes.

"You did, Parker. You make me cry because you touch my heart. These tears heal me." His tenderness erased the ugliness of what she had known in her previous marriage. He showed her respect, care, protection and love.

"Nina, I love you."

Her name always felt poetic in his deep voice. "I love you too, Parker. Until death do us part."

The rays of the sun from the new day illuminated the couple. Nina was rediscovering her lost identity, the one she had received at conception. The pain had drained her, but it hadn't destroyed her essence—it had been hidden beneath the shell of sadness caused by violence, but had been gradually restored by grace. It was not a definitive happily-ever-after. It was a process, she was convinced. The choices were to let bitterness weigh her down in a sea of resentment or to allow grace to wash away the scars caused by Anderson.

Nina chose grace.

In her husband's arms, she surrendered her heart once again. She dove into the sea of the most tender affections and delightful caresses.

It was good. It was right. The love she had for Parker, and he for her, confirmed that.

***

"That's a low blow." Parker scooped up a handful of damp sand and tossed it onto her legs while wrestling with his yellow kite.

Nina dashed on the sand, where the waves came in and out, leaving foam and pushing shells along the shore. Her blue rain boots traced her path as she flew the colorful kite. With the wind playing with her curly locks, she felt like she was also flying.

She was free. She was free!

"Next time, keep your kite away from mine," she shouted, jumping over a small wave and splashing salty water around.

"Oh, that's war?" Parker tugged on the line a few times, sending his kite diving through the air. He ran backward, eyes on the sky, bringing his yellow kite closer to hers.

"You've just declared war." Nina spun around and sprinted, managing the line as she pulled away from Parker.

The competition continued until Nina and Parker surrendered to exhaustion. They tucked away the kites and strolled hand in hand along the water's edge, the only ones on that secluded stretch of beach. The cottage perched on the rocks seemed to keep a watchful eye over them with its wide, welcoming windows.

Nina unbuttoned her yellow rain jacket, letting the sea air dry her sweaty body. Parker pulled his wife closer.

"Missing home?" he asked.

Home. Nina and Parker had bought a house next to Tranquility-by-the-Sea Inn weeks before their wedding. They'd decorated it with the help of Jade, who insisted on a marine-themed décor. Their niece gave them a painting of the sea with kites in the sky as a gift. The painting stood out on the living room wall. Nina and Parker's house was small and cozy, with its own personality. It was their space to welcome friends and family, to care for one another. "A home with open doors," Nina had said to Parker when he shared how Jade was feeling down about her uncle's move. She wanted their home to embrace those in need of comfort.

Nina wrapped her arm around Parker's. "I can't wait to start our life together."

He stopped and turned her to face him. "We've already started."

As the soothing sound of the waves filled the air, Nina felt Parker lean in, meeting her lips in a long, deep kiss. It was a moment suspended in time, where the world around them faded away, leaving only the warmth of their relationship.

Yes, her life was beginning, built on the foundations of faith, grace, and love.

THE

END